ONE,
BEYOND TIME

Gates McKibbin

CONTENTS

DEDICATION

My mother was an avid reader of romance novels. She delayed applying for a library card until my youngest brother was in school, since she knew that once she dipped into a paperback she would never accomplish everything a family of seven needed her to do. Two of her preferred authors were my favorites as well. We spent hours on the phone recounting what we enjoyed most about their latest releases (gloriously male protagonists included).

Mother isn't here to read the stories in the *Love Hope Give* series, but I dedicate them to her nonetheless. They aren't what she typically checked out of the library, but she might still have enjoyed the adventures of Grace and Luke.

FOREWORD

The four novels in the *Love Hope Give* series arrived over a two-year period when I was living among ancient redwoods in Marin County, California. Whenever I had a free day on a weekend I would park myself on the sofa with a blank journal and a pen, ready to write whatever came through me. By the end of the day the pages would be spilling over with words, most of which I couldn't recall.

I never learned to type without looking at the keyboard – a particularly fraught process when handwritten material must be entered into the computer. So I used voice recognition software to transfer the narratives from my journals onto the hard drive. Reading each novel aloud was a fascinating process, since I had no idea what would happen next. I discovered the story arcs not as I was writing them, but as I was reading them afterward.

I shared early drafts with a few friends. One of them who lives in Portland told me a portrait caught her eye when she was visiting the art studio of her friend Serena Barton. It had an uncanny resemblance to how she envisioned Grace in the first novel *One, Beyond Time*. When we visited the studio a few weeks later, Grace was indeed waiting for us.

Serena gave me permission to use the portrait on my book cover. She also agreed to create artwork for the other three novels. As I was describing the storyline in *Love, 24 AD* she stopped me saying, "I may have a few pieces that would work." She hopped on a stool and retrieved three canvases from an upper shelf. "How about these?"

Incredibly, Serena had captured Grace in her three subsequent incarnations even though she knew nothing about the stories. Clearly she and I had connected in the realms beyond time and space. I purchased all four portraits on the spot.

May the *Love Hope Give* series fill your heart with your own deep inner knowing that anything is possible when love is your guiding light.

PART ONE
GRACE AND LUKE

You are my one and only love, the one I long for wherever I am, the one who completes me. You are my eternal complement carrying within you the potential for me to become whole, for us to become whole, for us to become one.

We begin again, just as we did so long ago when you and I were one then split into two. That was a beginning for each of us as separate spirits, souls apart, suddenly but not irrevocably. At the time it seemed more like an ending than a beginning. But that was then, and this is now. And now we are about to begin anew.

We were once one spirit, incarnating as an androgynous being in Lemuria and then Atlantis, dedicated to the evolution of consciousness in the context of the human condition. We – or perhaps I should say "that person," for we as two did not yet exist – were fulfilled and content. Resonance with the Divine came effortlessly. The lifetimes this spirit incarnated on Earth were blessed.

Between lifetimes and just before the one being recounted in this volume, this spirit attended a gathering of its soul group in the nether realms. Archangelic presences joined us, emanating love as only they can do. It was an auspicious occasion, although no one knew its purpose or the insights to be imparted.

Archangel Michael stepped forward, declaring, "The fundamental illusion standing between divine grace and fallen consciousness is the belief that lovelessness is real. We are about to launch an experiment on planet Earth that will test the ability of spirits in human embodiment to find their way back to oneness with their Creator after they encounter separateness.

"This separateness will be accomplished through the splitting of one spirit into two spirits that will take embodiment many times over. Initially they will experience the perfect gender complementarity of the masculine and feminine. Over time and using free will as the foundation principle for all choice, those spirits will move toward either greater differentiation or greater oneness. That we cannot predict. But if it is the former, the road will be fraught with the compelling illusions and disquieting manifestations of a fall from grace.

"If this experiment leads to a fall, it will nonetheless hold great promise that humankind might consistently choose the light over seductions of the fallen. In doing so each person expands the potential for all to see the light, evolve toward the light and live in the light.

"It is an epic journey, this path from darkness into light. And it starts within each spirit, always and forever. One spirit at a time rediscovers the Divine within. One spirit at a time comes face-to-face with its fundamental essence, which is all love and all loving."

What Archangel Michael imparted to us was familiar to each spirit attending the gathering. It was the story of Creation: being born into grace, losing one's way then finding it again. What made the circumstances on Earth unique?

Michael apprehended our silent questions and responded. "The experiment on Earth is being conducted in the context of gender complementarity. Not just humans will be male or female; all of life will be.

"Those of you who participate will take embodiment as one spirit, one genderless person. During that lifetime you will have the opportunity to use your free will choice to split into two spirits – two people, a male and a female. Initially your DNA blueprints will be identical, except for what differentiates the two genders.

"You will experience many lifetimes as two distinct individuals, remaining in relative contact with each other in and out of embodiment. Then in a lifetime that one or both of you experience on Earth, you will merge again into oneness. This gift will be made available only after you have earned it, after you have faced many trials and proven your capacity to be and see the Divine in all that is.

"This is a challenging path. It can also be extraordinarily rewarding and fulfilling. Inherent in it is the potential not just for the two of you to become one again, but also for your shared spirit to evolve into oneness with your Creator. Even more expansively, you stimulate the potential for all spirits in human embodiment to move toward oneness and, beyond that, for all of Creation to become one again in love.

"This is a request, not a requirement. Whatever you choose, you will contribute to the progression of consciousness. You are loved. All is well."

As I listened to these messages emanating from Michael, I discerned that I would become involved in this experiment. It was not that I longed for something new – a grand adventure, a rite of passage that would take me to an expanded level of divine understanding. Rather, I had just glimpsed my own unfolding. Whatever interruptions and detours lay ahead, I would be of service. That was all I needed to know.

Soon afterward I received the blueprint for my next lifetime on Earth. I established that after my twenty-third birthday I would have the option of taking part in this experiment, which would require the most advanced technology and spiritual practice to split one spirit into two. It was not unlike the process of splitting one atom into two.

Nothing was concluded then except my taking embodiment and navigating through various choice points. Since free will would be at work, the decisions themselves could not be predetermined.

∞　∞　∞

When the opportunity to transform from one into two was presented to me, I agreed to it.

Looking back on that crossroads, I am aware of both my wisdom and my innocence. The latter was essential, since without it I might well have declined the offer. It did not require extensive analysis to conclude I was about to take a foolhardy leap into the unknown. And I was anything but foolhardy.

Nonetheless, one afternoon I entered the chamber where the split was to occur in a sacred chapel of the Temple of the Central Sun. Priests and priestesses of the highest order were present, each who had once been one unified spirit.

The chamber was arranged to reflect all aspects of divine complementarity in material form. At the center on a platform of quartz crystal was an imposing eight-pointed, three-dimensional structure called a Merkabah, also constructed of crystal. I entered the Merkabah, a genderless being for the last time.

As the priests intoned the voices of the angels, the priestesses chanted a complementary vibration. I welcomed the ardor in their chanting, imbibed the intoxicating fragrance of the burning incense, focused my mind on selfless service and surrendered.

My spirit floated tentatively above my body then gradually abandoned it completely, remaining within the Merkabah. I wondered if I was about to undergo a physical death instead of a split into two. Rather than being alarmed at that possibility, I was enveloped in serenity.

Suddenly a blinding flash of high frequency light penetrated my being, sending a powerful shock that disintegrated my body. I assumed I had died in the Merkabah, the victim of a disastrously failed experiment. Even then I was at peace. If my life ended, so be it.

A deeper calm descended upon me, and I prepared to return to the higher realms as I had done in prior physical deaths. I surrendered more completely.

As the complementarity of the vibrations emanating from the chanting achieved perfect harmony, my spirit entered the void of divine consciousness. Neither a thought nor an expectation defined me. The blessed emanation of Source enfolded my essence. I welcomed the homecoming.

The last vestiges of what I had come to know as "myself" were gone. I was not even a unique spirit. I had no means of affirming definitively "I am."

Whatever constituted my being was embraced by divine love. And in that moment I experienced a re-emergence into two spirits. I had been one, then no one. Then I became two.

I fully occupied one of the two spirits. The other was familiar to me but was not I. Gazing upon the spirit of my complement, I felt such a strong connection, I knew I had just met my eternal beloved.

I was barely acquainted with my split self – the half the new "I" occupied – when I was thrust back into the Merkabah. My spirit hovered over the body of a woman.

My complement's spirit floated above the body of a man. Two of us manifested not just in the realms of the Divine but also on the Earth plane as a man and a woman.

Waves of unconditional love pulsed between our spirits, and for a moment we merged into one again. I was ecstatic. Never before had I experienced the joy of such union. Then just as quickly we separated, and our spirits entered our new physical bodies for the first time.

How odd to be a female after knowing only androgyny! I can't say I was pleased with the change. It felt rather like being a rose then suddenly finding oneself to be a dove.

This would take some getting used to.

∞ ∞ ∞

I recall my first night as a spirit in female embodiment as if it occurred just yesterday. I was taken to the Temple of the Divine Feminine and shown to my room, decorated in subtle hues of turquoise and mauve with doors opening onto a garden. I was to reside there during my transition from androgyny to the female gender. After that I could decide whether to remain in the temple or create a life in the outside world.

Maya, the temple priestess assigned to assist me, explained, "You have no experience embodying a gender. It is as if you have been dropped into a foreign culture.

"Before you can be effective as a woman, you must learn what it means to be female. Your physical body has a different purpose now. You have the structure and tides of a woman. You can create life and experience cycles in resonance with the waxing and waning of the moon. You can merge physically with another so completely you lose yourself in love. You contain the receptive power of the divine feminine in all her aspects."

"How will I ever become accustomed to these changes?" I asked, unable to hide my concern.

"It will take a while for you to integrate this limited yet limitless sense of self," Maya replied. "It is limited in that you are now defined by a gender. It is limitless in that the divine feminine has infinite power to create in the context of the divine love within you."

"How can I embrace that power?" I persisted.

"You will be taught the ancient secrets of your divinity as a woman," she explained. "You will learn how to be selfless and all-seeing, wise and humble, courageous and generous. You will discover what it means to be part of the eternal flow as a supremely differentiated being."

"But I don't see how this differentiation represents a positive change," I stated flatly. "I am terribly disoriented and not a little confused."

"I understand," Maya replied with compassion. "You are experiencing an intense longing unlike anything you have known before. So deeply will you hunger to merge with your divine complement, you will discount your gifts. Over lifetimes you may even forget you ever had a complement. You will look for him in others, a singularly unfulfilling proposition. Despite those detours, you will be on a path that returns you to oneness with his spirit. It is inevitable."

"This shift is so extreme, I doubt we will ever find our way back to oneness," I worried.

"Rest assured you will," Maya said softly. "And when you do, all the trials you experience along the way will be well worth the journey."

The overwhelming consequences of my choice to become two descended upon me in an avalanche of fear and regret. Loneliness, a uniquely foreign emotion, hit me like a frigid wind from the north.

I was alone, separated from a part of my spirit that now resided within another person whom I knew intimately and did not know at all. This individual had become a "he" to my "she." Would he recognize me? And if so, would he like me, let alone love me? Would he even care that I existed?

These questions haunted me as I fell asleep on my first night as a woman.

∞ ∞ ∞

It is hard to say how long I slept, but at one point I felt my spirit leaving my body and traveling to find him. I searched without a map or a plan, using my connection with him to guide my travels. I kept telling myself he could not have gone far or have changed all that much in such a short time.

My spirit was returning to the temple, where my body lay in contented repose, when I felt an approaching magnetism so forceful, my initial reaction was to elude it. Never had I known such a pull toward another. It was more threatening than affirming.

I gathered my energy and the magnetism diminished. In the stillness my beloved other appeared gently and with great consternation.

"Were you hiding from me?" he asked.

"No, I simply quieted my being so I could identify who or what was pursuing me," I replied.

"You didn't recognize me, then?" he clarified.

"The force of your impulse toward me was so great, I couldn't initially discern its source," I explained.

"And now that you have, are you still concerned?" he pursued.

"I am gratified we found each other," I assured him. "I went looking for you at the first opportunity. My body is still fast asleep, thank goodness. Let's use this time to discover each other."

"Those were my intentions exactly. But first, what is your name?" he asked. "I am Luke, by the way."

"And I am Grace," I replied, aware of the irony inherent in our introduction.

"Where are you living?" he asked.

"I am in the Temple of the Divine Feminine. It was determined, though I don't know how, that I belonged among those of the highest order," I remarked. "They are assisting with my transition into womanhood."

"What does that involve?" he asked.

"I am not altogether certain," I admitted. "I have little context for being a woman."

"Nor do I as a man. I am as lost as you are," he admitted. "I am living among the priests in the Temple of the Divine Masculine. Their intention is to prepare me to serve, whether or not I choose to enter the world."

"My circumstances are the same," I replied. "I can remain in the temple as a priestess if I want."

If a spirit can blanch, his did. That last comment clearly distressed him. I floated closer and whispered, "What have we done?"

"We have launched ourselves on separate courses that may not converge for a very long while," he responded quietly.

"How do you know that?" I wondered.

"Immediately after I realized the effect of the split, I petitioned to have it nullified," he replied. "I didn't believe I could withstand a lifetime, let alone multiple lives, longing for oneness with my beloved other – you. My petition was denied at once.

"There's no turning back. We've thrust ourselves into a living hell. I don't care about contributing to the evolution of consciousness if it means living with the ceaseless desire to merge with you."

"You speak from the shock of it all," I observed. "In time the longing will fade."

"I don't want it to fade!" he exclaimed. "Don't you see? My sole purpose is to return to you. I will not rest until we are one again. Expect me to pursue you wherever you are, and to be by your side any way I can. I will not survive without you. I don't want to survive without you."

I felt the intensity of his longing and speculated whether it derived from love or a reaction to the monumental shift that had just occurred. Then a surge of irresistible love for him obliterated all else. I was nothing but a woman who loved a man with every aspect of my being.

I enveloped Luke in that love. His spirit came to me with such relief and gratitude, I lapsed into ecstatic union with him. We remained together, vibrating as one yet aware we were two. I gave myself over to that love. It defined me. I was his divine complement, his eternal love, his reason for being, as he was mine.

Inevitably I felt our union waning. When we were fully separate, he whispered tenderly, "I'll come for you every night and often during the day. Our lives may be disconnected now, but our spirits remain capable of union in love.

"Our bond is love. Our shared existence is made possible by love. We come together eternally because of our love. There is no reality other than that love. Some day, some blessed moment in the tapestry of our divided existence, we will once again be one."

He enveloped me in his love before he departed. I was alone, contemplating who we would be when that oneness arrived. More immediately I wondered who I would be when the next day dawned.

I awoke with a gnawing hole in my being. How could I reclaim my dearest other if I had no way of claiming myself?

∞ ∞ ∞

My life in the temple alternated between development and discovery. I developed the capacities of the priestesses who taught me the secret rituals of their order. I also discovered the joys and responsibilities of being female.

I left the temple grounds infrequently, always accompanied by other priestesses. We visited distant healing centers and attended congregations with priests from our partner temple. Although I had been welcomed into an extended spiritual family, I felt little comfort or security. I constantly wondered how long I would remain in the temple, away from my beloved.

Were we to meet, I couldn't resist merging physically as well as spiritually with him. But such coming together had to be avoided, at least initially, since it would be an act of desperate desire for union rather than enlightened love. And so we were kept apart.

At night my spirit flew to meet him as soon as I fell asleep. We selected our favorite vortices for our rendezvous: the cliff overlooking a tempestuous ocean, a placid beach in a cove, the depths of a tropical forest where a hidden waterfall cascaded into a canyon. We had privacy there, unseen even by the spirits who traveled those circuits. Or we thought we were unseen. Actually, we were quite visible but were allowed our seclusion.

During the day my hunger to merge with him became so demanding, I couldn't concentrate on anything else. The night would arrive none too soon. Then as we slumbered apart from each other, our spirits united again in ecstatic relief.

We shared details of the previous day and taught each other what we learned. He described constructs through which men perceive the world. I began to understand their dynamism, the source of masculine power and physical capacity. I discovered the interplay between masculine forthrightness and feminine receptivity, and how they complement each other.

As the months unfolded, our worldly experiences occupied a greater portion of our days. Our lives increasingly diverged, creating cracks where there once was unity.

One night after our spirits met I was stunned when he asked, "Do you still love me?"

"Of course I do," I replied. "Why do you raise such a question?"

"We've lost something, and I'm not sure how to recapture it," he revealed.

"You are my other half, my beloved for all eternity," I assured him. "Our paths may vary at times, but you are always with me – a part of me."

Gazing into his vibration, I recognized a facet I hadn't seen before: sorrow over an apparently irretrievable loss. His longing had become a pain so wrenching, it threatened to tear his spirit apart. I wanted to save him, not just comfort him. But I could not.

I could love him with all my being. I could offer support and sustenance in myriad ways. But I could neither interfere nor intercede on his behalf. I couldn't keep him from himself.

"I feel you drawing away from me again," he said.

"Oh, my love, it's the opposite," I whispered. "There is no limit to my love, but there are limits to the degree to which I can live your life. In fact, I can't live your life. Although I am your perfect complement and you are mine, I am not you."

I declared that knowing full well that what he desperately wanted was to return to our original oneness, when I *was* he.

A part of him was missing. The more I tried to convince him of my love, the more he retreated into his longing to become one spirit again. Rather than being an affirmation of what he had, my love was a constant reminder of what he was missing.

Here is the crux of the matter: The two of us were approaching our new existence in fundamentally different ways. I accepted it for what it was, unfamiliar and untested though it might be, and tried to accommodate the shifted parameters of my being. I found a natural flow and remained within it, not because I had given up, but because it was the most appropriate approach to my altered circumstances. I am not hinting I was better than he – only that I accepted the realities of the feminine earlier in the process.

He, on the other hand, was in male embodiment, learning the dynamics of masculine intention and purpose. Whereas my challenge was to find the flow and follow it, his was to confront the current reality and improve it.

The aspect he rejected immediately and completely was the condition of being only half of his former self. He wanted wholeness, oneness. He wanted to turn back time to when we were one and never again consider the alternative. He wanted not just me, not just my love, but also our reunification.

That was not possible. And so he grieved.

∞   ∞   ∞

In the beginning of this lifetime, when Luke and I were one androgynous person, that individual's purpose was to heal misalignments in the physical body that resulted in disease. This was accomplished through the integration of ancient spiritual practices and highly advanced technologies. Working together, these forces could shift the vibratory frequencies embedded in the physical body at a cellular level.

Healing resulted when cells cleansed of low-frequency emanations pulsed in perfect harmony with the Divine. Under those conditions one could remain healthy and live vitally until the lifetime was completed. Death occurred not as a result of the wearing out of the physical body, but because there was no further reason for the spirit to remain in its current incarnation.

The person we were before was associated with a group of scientists and priests collaborating to take this work to higher levels. They were creating innovative approaches to the ongoing revitalization of cells to prevent deterioration. People could then thrive without additional intervention.

Other experiments were occurring as well. Diversity was blossoming where homogeneity once prevailed. Gender-based splits were occurring frequently. This could be accomplished so precisely nothing from the original encoding was lost or reprogrammed. Much had changed, apparently for the better.

But many felt the risks outweighed the potential benefits. Weren't such splits more likely to lead to conflict and corruption than harmony and complementarity?

Perhaps so. But one evening during meditation I entered a Merkabah of golden light. A pervasive peace descended upon me. Without warning my entire being shattered, transforming from one into two. I had become "they" – unimaginable and absolutely real.

In the months that followed I had similar meditative experiences. I witnessed the two people I had become, a man and a woman, as they proceeded with their lives. It was like reading a spiritual tome and a romantic saga rolled into one.

Walking on the beach one afternoon, I realized I was viewing my own future as two people – a man and a woman. I had been given glimpses into what lay ahead if I agreed to participate in the gender experiment. It was at once inspiring and daunting.

I could either pursue the known course of my life as I planned and engineered it, or I could set that aside and leap into the unknown. I chose the latter.

I prepared for my transformation as if for a death. I gave my most precious belongings to family and friends and arranged to have my estate divided equally between the two people I would become. I left nothing to reveal who I had been before the split. I said goodbye to those most dear to me and prepared for my leave-taking.

On my way to the temple where the transformation was to occur, I felt alternately apprehensive and exhilarated. The priests and priestesses involved were enlightened adepts, yet so much could go awry. I held fast to the visions I experienced during my meditations. My prayer was that the twin souls I was about to become would eventually reunite in love eternal.

He is tall, with thick dark hair, broad shoulders and piercing gray eyes that are open windows into his heart. He emanates profound sensitivity and equally deep compassion. Looking at him, one senses he is a very old soul, a wise man somewhat disoriented in the culture in which he finds himself. Love cascades from him like a vessel overflowing with wine. But that love also bespeaks a melancholy, as if loving has ushered in exquisite loss. He is a handsome man, humble yet imposing, defined by his complexities.

She is his opposite, short in stature and sassy in temperament, though her hair and eyes are also dark. She is a realist, able to size up a situation quickly and discern the most appropriate course of action, the better to handle it and move on. Whereas he is contemplative, she is more at ease taking a step, observing what happens and changing course accordingly.

∞ ∞ ∞

We had not met face-to-face. He was aware of what I looked like, and I would have recognized him in a crowd. But we were not allowed to journey to any location where the other might be physically present. Our coming together at night became ever more desperate as I tried to comfort him and he spoke only of the longing in his soul.

One day as I meditated in my room, a priestess knocked on my door and announced that a visitor was waiting in the garden designated for men and women to meet.

I passed the lily pond and followed the stone path to the curved wall blossoming with bougainvillea. Then I saw him at a distance, his back turned to me. I was glued to the spot, transfixed, breathing in staccato bursts.

Seeing him in the flesh, I experienced a rush of love inconceivably whole unto itself, making me whole. My love for him completed me, even though we were two.

This was an altogether different experience from how our spirits merged when we slept. It derived from the magnetic desire of two people to mate, to become one in physical union.

He turned slowly and walked toward me, drinking in my presence as if he had thirsted for it since the birth of his being. And in truth he had. I welcomed his advances, feeling a quickening at my core that spoke insistently of my own longing.

Standing before me he took my face in his hands and kissed it, my eyes first, the tip of my nose, my mouth gently and then more passionately. We embraced, locking the length of our bodies together as we stood with the sun glistening and the bees gathering their nectar.

"We meet at last," he whispered. "I've thought of this moment ever since you appeared opposite me in the Merkabah. Nothing I imagined compares with the actual you."

"But you have met the actual me," I reminded him, "every night, as I recall."

"Just as your spirit has been my constant companion, I want you as my constant companion in person," he declared. He was being consummately masculine, resolute and focused on achieving a purpose.

I appreciated and even applauded his decisiveness. But did I not have a voice in the matter? Was it not my choice as well to be his constant companion in the outside world? Although his certainty was compelling, I had grown accustomed to the serenity and solitude of the temple.

Nonetheless, I could neither imagine nor accept the possibility of being with anyone but him. As long as we walked the planet at the same time, he would be my love. He completed me when we came together in spirit. Why question how he might complete me in the physical?

I savored his arms around me, his heart pulsing against my cheek. I gave myself over to him. My beloved had come for me, and I was ready to make a life with him.

We discussed how we might enter the world as a couple and make our way side-by-side. We could live together, spend every night in the same bed and create a union in every way short of the impossible – becoming one spirit again.

"So you'll go away with me?" Luke asked.

"I may not be allowed to," I replied. "We've been kept apart until now."

"When I petitioned to see you, I also requested permission to leave with you if that's what you want," he revealed. "We have the blessing of both temples to create a life together if we so choose."

I was heartened by who Luke had become – optimistic, self-assured, determined. The combination was persuasive and, not incidentally, quite seductive.

"I'll leave with you, my love, as soon as you have found a place for us to live," I replied. "A simple room is good enough."

"In two days' time I'll come for you," Luke announced. "When I see you next, it will be to take you to our home."

As I was about to express doubts that he could locate even a room for rent by then, he halted my questioning with a splendidly thorough kiss. I was undone. This man could take me away whenever, wherever.

"Agreed?" he asked, eyes twinkling.

"Agreed," I replied, flushed and more than a little discombobulated.

He kissed me on both cheeks, embraced me enthusiastically and departed.

I said goodbye to the priestesses I had come to know, expressing my gratitude for their assistance. They assured me I made the right choice to be with Luke and mentioned we would be meeting again. When I asked for details, they replied enigmatically that I would find out when the time came.

∞ ∞ ∞

Luke and I departed from the temple on a sunny morning full of promise. Transportation was waiting outside to take us to a beachside neighborhood. We stopped at the gate leading to a small cottage near the ocean, in the shadow of the renowned Temple of the Central Sun.

"This is ours?" I exclaimed.

"It is," he said simply.

"It's lovely! How did you find it so quickly?" I asked.

"My mentor in the temple just happened to know of a couple who had recently been transferred to another location, and they were looking for caretakers for their house," Luke explained. "He obtained their immediate approval for us to live here. We can remain until we find a place of our own or until they return, whichever comes first."

The house was what I would have envisioned had I dared hope for more than a barely furnished room with a bed (to be used a great deal, I imagined) and minimal necessities.

Luke walked me to the front door and turned the key in the lock. Inside the sun sparkled through the windows. Sliding doors off the main living room led to a deck overlooking the ocean. Flowers from the garden arranged in hand-blown vases accented furnishings that bespoke of informal luxury. We would be happy here.

The kitchen had been stocked with fresh food – Luke had thought of everything – so all I had to do was settle in.

That was easier said than done. How does one settle in with another who is both intimately familiar and not really known at all? The paradox of our immediate circumstances wasn't lost on me.

Nor was it on him. "Now what do we do?" he asked, smiling as brightly as the sun on the sea.

"Shall we try to navigate the kitchen together?" I suggested.

"I'm not all that hungry," he replied. "How about a walk on the beach?"

"I prefer to stay here and enjoy our new surroundings," I said.

"The library is full of interesting volumes, everything from esoteric metaphysical treatises to advanced scientific research," Luke revealed. "Shall we retire to the deck with a couple of good books?"

"Actually, I'm rather sleepy," I yawned as I spoke. "Want to take a nap?"

I surprised him with my casual invitation to join me in bed.

"A nap would be great," he agreed. "I've been so preoccupied getting ready for you, I barely slept."

When we walked into the bedroom, we looked at each other and burst out laughing.

"Which side do you want?" he asked.

"Either one is fine with me," I chirped.

"Me too," he replied amiably.

I noticed aromatic oils and lotions on one side of the bed, fragrances used in the Temple of the Divine Feminine. "Looks like that one is mine," I commented, pointing to the alabaster jars. He nodded casually.

We got into bed on our respective sides. I lay straight and stiff, making sure not to touch him. "I'll never be able to sleep this way," I thought, then turned on my side facing the outside edge of the bed and curled up. No sooner had I moved than he was behind me, tucked in close.

"Sweet dreams," he whispered. I fell asleep to the rhythms of his breathing.

Many hours later I felt him stirring and climbed out of a deep sleep. It was dark outside. I heard the ocean waves in their inexorable progression to the beach and savored his presence in bed with me.

I lay still for a while, familiarizing myself with him. Here was my divine other, the one who forever would complete me. Yet in many ways we were strangers. How should we proceed, now that we were living together under one roof?

"I want to wait until you are ready," he whispered as if in response to a question I asked. In truth he was doing just that, although I hadn't verbalized it.

"Thank you for that," I acknowledged gratefully. "I have no idea how to approach our impending intimacy."

"It needn't be impending," he replied, attempting to quell my discomfort. "I'm content just to live with you and hold you next to me. These are blessings I'll never take for granted. We can grow into our intimacy as we get to know each other."

I turned and faced him in bed. His hair was disheveled, his eyes still sleepy. But the love pouring from him was so pure and given so generously, all I could do was cry.

When my breathing returned to its regular rhythm, he kissed the top of my head. I nestled my cheek into his chest, burrowing deep as if to find a hibernating place for the winter. In the blissful embrace of my beloved, I slept through the night.

I awoke to dazzling sunlight piercing the windows and dancing around the room like a hummingbird amidst succulent blossoms.

"Good morning, my dearest Luke," I whispered. "This is our first day waking up together in our own place."

"Good morning to you, my sweet Grace," he responded. "And a wonderful day it is."

"Especially when it starts off in bed with you," I replied.

We played like puppies that morning, exploring a physicality that was altogether new to us. We needed to experience a brief bout of adolescence before we could enter into a more mature familiarity.

That afternoon a neighbor stopped by to introduce himself and tell us about the surrounding community. We had landed in an eccentric village – a vortex of alternative perspectives. When our neighbor invited us to a gathering of families living on our lane, we accepted.

That evening we perused the bookshelves – volumes on the appropriate use of high-vibrational frequencies and case studies of miraculous healing through a combination of prayer and advanced quartz crystal technology.

I selected a volume bound in burgundy leather with gold embossing entitled *Exploration of the Consequences of Free Will Choice on Spiritual Transcendence*. I mused that since I had become an active participant in such an experiment, I should learn more about it.

The sun had set before I was aware of anything other than the stories this book revealed. It chronicled the lives of others who preceded Luke and me, describing their sojourns after having split into two. Some accounts were exalted and inspiring; others were troubling and frighteningly full of warnings. Apparently after becoming two it was just as easy to lose one's way as it was to follow the path of spirit.

I searched for patterns leading to one course or the other. My sincerest hope was that we would not be tempted to abuse our powers as others had.

But what were those powers, exactly? If anything Luke and I might have diminished capacities. But then, we were just becoming acquainted with ourselves individually and with each other. It was too early to tell.

I was drawn to the fragrance of roasting vegetables and something delectable baking in the oven. Was I living with a marvelous man who could also cook? I hadn't set foot in a kitchen since I arrived as a female. Maybe he got the cuisine gene.

"I'm thrilled we have a chef in the family!" I exclaimed as I entered the kitchen, suddenly starving.

"I hardly qualify for chef status, but at least this will keep us from expiring due to malnutrition," he quipped.

"Seriously, how is it you know how to cook?" I asked.

"How is it we both know how to read and write?" he queried back. "I assume we brought forth abilities that were developed before, but I have no recollection of what they are."

"Nor do I," I noted.

"This is a discovery process," he observed. "Each day we can uncover what we know and what we don't understand, what we can and can't do, who we are and who we are not."

"So I can't try to convince you I'm better than I actually am," I laughed, "because I have no idea who I am. Besides, you see me more perceptively than I do myself."

"We do know a few things," he continued. "We know the person we used to be was a spiritual adept."

"How can we be certain of that?" I asked.

"Only those who embody the highest vibrations of divine essence are given the opportunity to split into complementary opposites," he explained. "While I was in the temple, a wizened priest explained why."

"Go on," I urged.

"Initially anyone was allowed to undergo the transformation," Luke explained. "Occasionally the person's fallen consciousness compromised the rituals, resulting in devastating misalignments. Even when the process was completed successfully, often the male and female who emerged were drawn to the dark side of their gender."

"I hope that doesn't happen to us," I commented.

"I doubt it. The priest told me he collaborated often with the individual. Apparently he was exceptional," Luke informed me.

"I agree, based on what's cooking in the kitchen," I teased. "No one swimming through the dregs of fallen consciousness could create such a delectable repast. Let's eat."

Dinner was even more delicious than I anticipated.

"How did you manage to prepare such sumptuous fare, given that we just arrived and as far as I know, you haven't left the house?" I wondered.

"I looked around, took a quick inventory of what was available, then gave my creative impulses the upper hand," he responded, smiling.

"I'm impressed," I declared. "I'll clean up."

∞ ∞ ∞

We fell into an effortless, natural daily rhythm. Already we had become best friends, candid and lighthearted. Together we developed a relaxed way for the days to unfold. I had few preoccupations, aside from my ongoing explorations in the library.

Just before we departed for the gathering at our neighbor's house, I asked Luke, "We have no history. What will we tell them about who we are and what we do?"

"They're aware of where we live, and they will see how much we love each other," he noted. "That's all they need to know."

No one asked any awkward questions. We enjoyed the evening, hearing stories about our neighbors and their daily lives.

Most of the adults were affiliated with an institute doing research on the transformation of consciousness toward oneness with Source. Some were masters in the arts of alchemy; some did scientific research on the realignment of brain waves during meditation; some measured the effect of thought forms on physical health; some were documenting the lives of people who existed for centuries, aging hardly at all. By the end of the evening Luke was invited to visit the institute. He agreed to do so the following week.

On the way home, Luke commented, "Did you notice anything unusual about everyone?"

"Besides being gracious and welcoming?" I asked.

"They are all couples like us," he noted. "I'm relatively certain they began the way we did. Many of them are working at the institute because the experiments there are unique to their situation, and now ours."

"That makes sense," I said. "Might one of us get involved with the institute as well?"

"Anything is possible," he replied casually.

We walked into our cottage and a new dimension of our lives, although we didn't know it quite yet.

∞ ∞ ∞

I continued to explore the extensive library collection. Some volumes challenged my thinking to such an extent I put them down after a quick perusal. Other manuscripts seemed more like fiction than fact. Those I set aside to dip into later.

The volumes making no pretense about being scientific felt the most authentic to me. They acknowledged no experimental validation, purporting instead to have been communicated by beings beyond the Earth plane. I was fascinated by the insights they revealed. Along the way I wove my own evolving tapestry of insights and questions.

Luke accompanied various neighbors doing research at the institute. He arrived home at the end of each day as full of ideas and queries as I was. We conducted our own informal institute every evening.

"Today I attended a seminar on reincarnation," Luke informed me. "It dealt with the capacity of one spirit to take human embodiment multiple times, during different eras, in either gender."

"I've been reading about that as well," I replied. "Each lifetime produces memory imprints on the vibrational essence of the soul, which then influence subsequent incarnations. The purpose of a lifetime is to provide opportunities to make choices that cleanse unwanted residue until the spirit is pristine, returning to oneness with Source."

"Are you sure you weren't a fly on the wall today?" he quipped. "That's exactly what the group discussed."

"And their conclusions?" I inquired.

"There's not enough evidence to reach a valid conclusion," he observed wryly.

"What did you conclude?" I wondered.

"It's strange. I experienced similar conversations during my past and future lifetimes," Luke revealed. "In each one I was a different person, except that I was also essentially the same as I am now."

"Sounds like reincarnation to me," I reasoned. "I wonder, though, whether memories of other lifetimes might be vulnerable to the power of suggestion."

"The feeling was real. The only thing more real to me, more real than anything I will ever know, is my love for you," Luke affirmed, his voice deep with feeling. "We'll know many lifetimes. Sometimes we'll be on Earth together, sometimes not. We may be lovers or friends. We may be of the same gender. We may be acutely aware we are divine complements, or not aware of it at all. Never will we be enemies, nor will we work at cross-purposes. Each lifetime will present situations that allow our spirits to grow together or further apart. And eventually – God I hope this is true – we'll earn the blessing of becoming one spirit once again."

"I pray that is possible," I replied.

"The potential is there," he assured me. "Whether we achieve oneness is up to us."

"How do we do that?" I asked.

"We start by committing to our eternal love," he whispered, looking at me intently, "and by doing everything we can to recognize each other wherever we are, between lifetimes or during them, whatever the circumstances. Our love transcends all outward appearances. If we hold that in our hearts, eventually we'll grow closer together until there is no difference between us."

"So it's all about the power of love to rise above everything else," I concluded.

"That's the one simple truth in a vast array of complexities," he declared.

"Let's get started, then!" I exclaimed.

"Doing what?" he asked.

"Imprinting our oneness onto all that we are," I answered.

I took Luke's hand and led him into the bedroom. The sun cast golden beams into the room.

"No need for candles," I mused.

I kissed him with a tenderness that soon became passionate – an undeniable longing to be physically one with this man. I was driven by a compelling need for completion.

Luke had something else in mind. "Let's take our time," he suggested.

"Why go slowly?" I asked.

"I've been waiting for you, anticipating our coming together. It's always slow and sweet, like a peaceful stroll on the beach. You want breakers crashing against cliffs. We'll get to that."

"Lead me, then," I whispered. "Help me find my way to you."

I brought his hand to my cheek, igniting the magnetism between us. I closed my eyes, took a deep breath and tried to calm my racing heart.

We stood holding each other. I wasn't sure what to do next. Though the priestesses had explained the physical and spiritual aspects of lovemaking with a male partner, I was adrift. My previous desire for union gave way to shyness.

"Now you understand why I wanted to go slowly," Luke whispered knowingly. "You'll be exquisite whenever we make love. I've seen it. The union we create – the seductive, spirited, sacred way we come together – will imprint on our individual spirits the inevitability of our final union many millennia from now."

"Hold me then," I said, "and help me get used to the idea."

We undressed, crawled into bed together, and I tucked my body into his. I dozed off, our hearts pulsing together. He stirred and I awoke slowly, experiencing his raw physicality.

"Do you have any idea how much I love you?" he murmured, his lips brushing mine. "I can't imagine living apart from you. If I had my way, we'd never leave this bed. You'd never leave my arms. I'd hold you so close, you'd melt into me, become me. Nothing would separate us."

"But we *are* together, just as you desire," I answered.

"I know," he continued. "But you'll not always be at my side. Many lifetimes will separate us, and sojourns between lifetimes will take us to realms distant from each other. What we have now is the exception, and it won't last long. I miss you already, and you haven't gone anywhere."

"We'll always come together again," I insisted. "We'll find each other."

The next morning I awoke alone in bed. In the kitchen was a breakfast tray for me, with a rose in a bud vase, a bowl of fresh fruit and a note that read: "Gone on a few errands. Back by evening. Enjoy your day. L"

I headed to the beach with a jug of water, a writing instrument and a blank journal from the library shelves. I sensed it was as important for me to document my own story as it was to read that of others, though I had no idea what I would say.

I found a secluded spot among the dunes, opened the journal and prepared to write. Nothing happened. No words came to mind. I closed my eyes and listened to the waves lapping against the shore.

Suddenly I began witnessing a conversation between Luke and myself. He was speaking with profound sadness and sincerity. My heart ached. I responded, but I couldn't discern what I had to say.

"Tell him yes," I begged. "Tell him you'll do everything in your power to find him when you are lost from each other. Tell him you'll be with him always, his one true love throughout lifetimes and in between. Tell him you're devoted to him and the promise of your oneness regained. Tell him that! Tell him!"

I saw myself communicate those words. He smiled slowly, relaxing, as did I.

I opened my eyes just as two birds flew overhead and then dived into the water for their next meal. I glanced at the empty journal and began writing what I saw in my vision.

The description flowed into a longer narrative. Rather than thinking about what I wrote, I allowed the story to tell itself. It was as if I were listening to a minstrel weaving an extemporaneous yarn. I wrote for hours, remembering hardly anything that unfolded on the pages.

Late that afternoon I returned home. Luke was sitting in the garden, brooding. I discarded an impulse to tell him about my writing. I stood behind him, placing my hands on his shoulders and massaging the tension from them.

"Whatever were you doing today to cause such distress?" I asked straight out.

"I was looking for work, for a way to support us," he replied.

"We don't need to worry about money," I observed. "A significant sum was left to us. We live so simply, it should last a long time."

"What about the inevitable purchases you'll want to make, so this house can be more a reflection of you?" he asked.

"I love this house as it is," I assured him.

"But it won't always be available to us," he continued. "At some point we'll have to move or want to buy a place of our own. We'll need resources to do that."

"True, but I can earn those resources as well," I asserted. "I want to do more than stay here all day reading and writing."

"Writing?" he wondered.

"Today an amazing thing happened," I revealed. "I went to the beach with a blank journal, had an arresting vision and decided to record it. Hours and dozens of pages later, I documented far more than the vision."

"Who are the main characters?" he asked.

"We are," I replied.

"You're telling our story? Share it with me," he suggested.

"Unfortunately, I don't recall many of the details," I admitted.

"Then I can't ask you if it has a happy ending," he quipped.

"It has a happy beginning, middle and end," I replied, coming around to face him. "By the way, not a word of fiction can be found in it."

"Could I see the volume, not to read it but to hold it?" he requested.

"Of course," I said, handing it to him.

"Look, a Merkabah is embossed on the cover," he observed.

"An essential component of the story, though I needn't tell you that," I replied. "This afternoon I saw in the Merkabah a pair of geometries coming together. It is us: two people in perfect harmony."

Luke held the volume in both hands, closed his eyes and revealed, "When we are one again, a long time from now, we'll come across this volume. It will have been preserved across the ages, a timeless text of legendary proportions. We'll read it and remember each chapter, each lifetime, as if it were yesterday. Thank you for recording this, for telling our story."

I vowed to myself and to him that I'd write every word that came to me, then put the narrative out of my thoughts. In the ensuing months I captured adventure after adventure, lifetime after lifetime, in the stories pulsing through me. Each day I awoke anxious to return again to the blank pages. And in the evening I closed the journal, grateful for the scenarios that unfolded before me. I blessed them all with love.

∞ ∞ ∞

Luke burst into the house one afternoon just as I was slicing plumbs and pears for a quick snack. "The most amazing thing happened this morning," he exclaimed. "I was on my way to the temple to meditate when I bumped into a neighbor who works at the institute. He's doing research on the influence of thought, feeling and prayer on the physical body. He told me they have an opening for someone to observe the research, monitor results and report conclusions. When he asked if I'd like to learn more about the position, I jumped at the chance."

"What did you find out?' I asked excitedly.

"His research center is in a small but comfortable building on the edge of the institute," Luke explained.

"Inside are meditation spaces, screening rooms and consultation chambers. Each one has a different purpose, but they are all focused on sending various stimuli to the brain and tracking their impact on the physical body. Quite intriguing. By the end of the day I had the job."

"Keep your eyes open for a possible position for me as well," I suggested.

"What about your writing?" he asked.

"That won't last indefinitely," I predicted. "When I've written all there is to say, I'll be anxious to pursue something else equally compelling."

"I can't promise anything at the institute would be as compelling as your stories," he chuckled, "but I'll serve as your advocate nonetheless."

"When can I accompany you?" I wondered. "I'd love to observe the research and perhaps even participate in some of the experiments."

"We'll see about that," he responded. "I don't want to lose you to a few well intentioned studies gone wrong."

"Do you have doubts about what they are doing?" I asked, surprised at his last comment. "Perhaps you should reconsider getting involved."

"It's too early to tell whether the work is principled and ethical, especially with regard to long-term effects on those participating in the experiments," Luke replied.

"Who are they?" I pursued.

"The institute involves people who can't find any other way to earn an income," he answered. "I want to make sure they are protected during the experiments and afterward. The inputs they receive must always be neutralized."

"How long do experiments last?" I asked.

"A minimum of six months," Luke replied. "But some people have been involved for years. They have dormitories for the more permanent participants."

"You may be observing how the research is progressing, but you'll also be watching out for those on whom the experiments are being conducted," I noted.

"Precisely," Luke affirmed. "I'm wondering how anyone can be consistently subjected to strong psychological inputs and not be affected by them. Granted, not all experiments are potentially problematic. The more enlightened ones involve meditation, mutual support, sharing and gratitude. But that is only half of the story. I intend to pay close attention to the other half."

"Maybe eventually you'll be documenting your own adventures," I commented, giving him a peck on the cheek. "In it you'll be the hero protecting the well-being of others."

"Don't make this more than it is," he cautioned. "For now it's just an occupation, to keep you well supplied with plums, pears and pomegranates."

"In that case, you're my hero as well," I laughed, giving him another kiss. But this time it was not on the cheek.

That kiss was infinitely more delectable than the fruits I had been savoring. In fact, it was so scrumptious I had to have another one, then another.

There we were, standing in the kitchen with ocean breezes wafting through the open door, kissing each other ardently. My body drew taut against his. I wanted every part of me as close to him as possible. I stood on tiptoes and pulled my face slightly from his, the better to look at him closely.

"I want you so much, I'm not sure I can endure another moment until we come together," I murmured.

"Nor can I," he whispered.

He swept me into his arms and carried me into the bedroom. I kissed his neck, his face, everything I had access to, my need for him consuming me.

He stood by the bed holding me and not moving a muscle. I quieted my kisses. Was he having second thoughts?

Just as I was about to plead with him that I really was ready to be his lover, he said softly, "I want to relish every aspect of this moment with you so I can remember it forever."

Gently he laid me on the bed, kissing me as he leaned over my body. An overwhelming love swept over me, leaving no room for anything else. Tears streamed from my eyes.

"I know," he whispered, kissing my tears away. "I love you that much as well."

Gazing into his eyes, I saw the pools of his being, the places where compassion and generosity, patience and courage dwelled. Oh, how I loved this man!

He kissed me softly as if to become reacquainted with me. I immersed myself in those kisses, trailing my fingers through his thick, dark hair. Our bodies undulated in the rhythms of the lovemaking to come, rising and falling together. I was aware of nothing but my beloved Luke.

He lifted himself off me and said, smiling, "Our clothes are getting in the way."

We sat up in bed and he unhooked the shoulders of my tunic, brushing his lips against my newly exposed skin. Sparks of longing quickened my desire. Slowly he undressed me.

"So beautiful," he whispered. "I want to explore every part of you."

I unfastened his robe and it fell to his waist. His shoulders were broad and muscled, perfectly proportioned. I sat astride his waist and ran my hands across his body, feeling his firmness and the down of hair covering it.

"And I'll take a very long time getting to know every inch of you," I crooned.

"I'm all yours," he declared. "Every inch of me."

"That's fortunate, because even if you weren't, I'd claim you anyway," I retorted. "There's no way I could allow you to slip through my fingers."

"Use your fingers any way you want," he smiled. "I won't fall through them, ever."

I covered his chest with my kisses, his hair tickling my cheek.

"You and I are so different, and yet we are exactly the same," I murmured. "We are two sides of one coin, two halves of the whole. We are love, separately and together. I didn't understand that until now."

I removed his robe, tossed it on a chair, and we lay down together. I settled my body along the length of his. Skin on skin, he was irresistible.

We moved with a shared cadence, matching each other's motions. We rode the swells of passion again and again, nearing climax and then allowing the ecstasy to subside, only to rekindle it once again.

We danced at the edge of orgasm until finally it became impossible to contain our desire for complete union. We climaxed together, wave upon wave, achieving the merging we both longed for.

My face was buried in his neck, his lips in my hair. We were wrapped around each other, satiated. I prayed to the goddess he would never leave and asked that even if he did, it wouldn't be for long.

"Shall we do this again sometime?" he murmured.

"Maybe, but only if you promise to be equally impressive, if not more so," I teased.

"That's a challenge, but I may be up to the task," he replied ironically.

We made love all over again, more slowly and luxuriously this time. I loved how he kissed me with a hunger that matched my own. I loved the deep reservoir of passion in his eyes, the hint of his lips on my skin, the groans of desire that accompanied his pleasure.

We slept in each other's arms, blissfully at peace and very much in love.

∞ ∞ ∞

Luke had already left for the institute when I arose the next morning. I recalled waking up just enough to receive his kiss goodbye before he was out the door.

I ached for him. The only way I would get through the day was to spend it writing at the beach. Tucked between the sand dunes, I was so absorbed in the story pouring through me I was unaware of my visitor until his shadow landed on my journal.

"Pardon the interruption, but I've seen you here for many weeks, always writing," he said by way of introduction. "Finally today I couldn't resist asking what you're creating. Can your life be so exciting, it takes hours on end to record it for posterity?"

"You'd be surprised," I deflected, recalling how Luke and I spent the night.

"Even if it is, you seem to be involved in more than that," he commented spiritedly. "For long periods of time you neither look up from the page nor stop writing."

It was disconcerting to learn he watched me so intently. The location I selected was private, which should have been evident to him.

"It's nothing, really," I responded, "just some rambling thoughts."

"There's not a shred of rambling in it," he observed.

Backlit he resembled a tall column that radiated light. When he stepped out of the sun, I realized I had seen him walking the beach before.

He wore a cream-colored robe made of light wool and bordered with an elaborately woven sea foam green-gray band. His light brown hair was in disarray, creating an unruly halo around his head. Blue-green eyes twinkled and danced. He was anything but intimidating.

"Why would it matter to you if I'm engaged in verbal wanderings or something more significant?" I inquired.

"I have more than a passing interest," he acknowledged. "I own a publishing concern, and we're always looking for the next great phenomenon to sweep the land. I thought perhaps you were creating something that would appeal to the masses."

"Why would you think that?" I wondered.

"Because clearly what you are writing is not coming from you," he declared. "In fact, no thought is involved in the process. If you approached what you are doing rationally, you would pause, edit, cross through a few lines, begin again and make slow progress. But you write so fluidly, there can be only one source for your material: your higher consciousness. Your intellect is completely disengaged."

"Wouldn't that make the narrative questionable?" I asked.

"Not at all," he assured me. "I've read many other manuscripts written this way, and they're invariably of better quality, more interesting and articulate, than the run-of-the-mill volume."

"I can't vouch for the quality of the story, because I have no idea what I'm writing," I confessed.

"You just proved my point," he declared with satisfaction.

"I guess I have," I admitted, "but that doesn't mean what has been flowing onto these pages would interest anyone but myself."

"I'd appreciate being the judge of that," he proposed.

"You want to read what I've written?" I inquired.

"Yes," he said simply.

"You'd be sorely disappointed," I cautioned.

"Why?" he pursued.

"Because it's just the story of this lifetime and those to come," I explained. "Nothing earthshaking."

"And what is more earthshaking than the human drama?" he asked pointedly.

"Very little if anything, I suppose," I answered. "Let me think about it, and we can talk again tomorrow."

"Good," he replied. "By the way, if I'm going to have access to your innermost musings, perhaps I should know your name."

"It's Grace," I told him.

"Hello, Grace. I'm Julian." He nodded, bowed ever so slightly, and turned to depart. "Until tomorrow, then."

I watched him as he walked away, following his slim, graceful outline moving along the edge of the water until it disappeared around the curve of the beach.

No sooner was he gone than I doubted the wisdom of showing him my writing. Even though I was fully engaged in the stories, they were lost to me the moment they arrived. For that reason alone, was it not imprudent to share the material with a stranger?

That evening Luke had a great deal to report, so I set aside my tale of the day's events.

"I'm alarmed by the experiments at the institute," he revealed. "I can't identify anything specific. But taken together, the impressions I got today make me wonder if I'm being shown the full picture."

"What's going on?" I asked.

"I can't say exactly," he replied. "The rooms where I do my work are pristine, the experiments are scientifically sound, and the participants are treated respectfully. The results seem to be recorded accurately and objectively.

"However, something totally different may be going on elsewhere. I'm being given access only to the experiments that pose little risk to the participants. They involve positive healing inputs such as meditation, supportive counseling and affirmations of human potential. But darker processes may also be occurring. Some people are like the walking dead. They seem mentally and psychologically destroyed."

"How do you know they didn't arrive that way?" I queried.

"I wondered that myself, so I asked to see the human subject selection criteria," Luke explained. "They are quite rigorous. Only those who are physically healthy and emotionally balanced are allowed into the program. The experiments would be invalid if the institute wasn't meticulous about the selection process. Everyone starts out the same so researchers can measure if they respond differentially to various inputs over time."

"You're suggesting that those whom you call the walking dead were well adjusted, functioning human beings when they arrived?" I asked.

"I believe they were," Luke verified. "But something in the experimentation process has destroyed them. I have to find out what it is."

There was a ferocity in his gaze I'd seen only once before, when he came to the temple garden to tell me of his desire to live with me.

"You must determine why these people are so disturbed," I agreed. "If there's no direct link with the experimentation, you can be assured ethical standards are in place. And if you uncover any irresponsibility or malevolence, you can root it out."

"That would be easier said than done," he observed. "But whatever I discover, I'll try to bring the situation to justice."

"Please be careful," I urged.

"No one will know of my suspicions," he assured me. "I'll build my credibility so I can gain greater access to information about the studies. I might even be able to enter the hidden wings of the facility, where I can determine what happened in the past and is probably still going on."

"Promise never to compromise your integrity to protect me," I urged.

"I promise," he said solemnly.

"And I promise never to ask you to put me before right action, whatever the cost," I vowed. "This I commit to you. I'll remember it always."

"And I'll love you always," he pledged.

Luke sat on the chaise and pulled me to him. I nestled into his lap, my face just under his chin and his arms around me securely. Soon I was asleep. Or perhaps I slipped into a wrinkle in time. I can't be certain.

I saw us saying goodbye to each other wordlessly. He was being silenced and taken to a nearby island, imprisoned for having challenged corrupt power. I watched the boat disappear beyond the horizon. Then I let out a wail. It came from deep within me, like a mama bear watching her cubs being massacred.

I returned to my body as Luke rocked me tenderly. If I had glimpsed the future, I wanted to retract the declaration I just made. Nothing was worth his imprisonment and potential loss of life. On the other hand, life was not worth living if it required sacrificing one's most fundamental values.

My eyes blinked open, colliding with Luke's worried look. "What just happened?" he asked urgently.

I willed myself to be truthful. "I saw you being taken away to a prison on an island," I revealed. "You exposed pervasive wrongdoing and as a result we were lost to each other. It was unbearable."

"But don't you realize we'll never be lost to each other?" he whispered reassuringly. "We may be separated, but that's only temporary. We'll always come back together, even after long absences. Knowing that will sustain us, whatever trials we face."

"You really believe that, don't you?" I asked. "How can you be so certain?"

"Our love is the source of my conviction and my courage," he declared.

Luke carried me into bed and laid me down gently. Lying in his arms, I slept soundly, dreaming. Each dream suggested a different lifetime when we would find each other under different – and often difficult – circumstances, always connected by our love.

I awoke to the sweet contentment of his arms enfolding me, his breath warm on my cheek. He stirred and asked, "Feeling better?"

"Yes," I assured him. "I dreamed of many lifetimes to come, all of them blessed with our love."

"And so, my dear, how shall we bless this one?" he inquired suggestively.

"Passionately," I murmured.

I felt his lips on mine, soft only momentarily and then fervent with anticipation. I melted into his kisses, not sure if he was devouring me or if I was devouring him. We seemed to be pulsing in and out of each other.

Luke framed my face in his hands, commenting, "I get lost in your love so easily, at times I feel I'll never find my way out. But then, I don't really want to. Even a kiss sends me deep within you. The last thing I want is to get myself back into control."

"Then don't," I urged.

I relaxed and savored his luxurious lovemaking. This would take a marvelously long time.

I fell asleep in his arms, the fragrance of our love thick in the air. My last thought was that this split into two wasn't so bad after all.

∞ ∞ ∞

I ended up not telling Luke about the conversation I had at the beach.

It's not that I wanted to keep it from him. Rather, my own activities seemed less relevant than his. I had only one question: Should I show Julian my manuscript? I answered it on my own. I would, but he would have to read it in my presence.

The next morning I went to the dunes at my usual time. My concentration was interrupted by thoughts of what Julian might say about my writing. Each time I returned to my story, refusing to let such concerns distract me for long.

Later that morning he appeared from behind the highest dune protecting me from view. "There you are," he said, not even pausing to say hello. "You're in a different location today. It's a good thing I let my intuition guide my feet. It seems to have worked."

"Seems so," I responded cheerfully.

"How do you want to proceed?" he asked.

"You're assuming I actually want to proceed," I replied. "That represents a rather large presumption."

"In this instance, I think not," he asserted.

"What would lead you to think that?" I pursued.

"You," was his simple declaration.

"You know nothing about me," I protested.

"And that, I might add, also represents a rather large presumption," he chuckled.

I took the bait. "So what do you know about me?"

"Do you really want to know what I know?" he challenged lightheartedly.

"Only what you know that I also know about myself," I cautioned. "I'm not ready for any surprises."

"Fair enough," he agreed. "Here is what I know about you. You are a messenger with a pure conduit from the higher frequencies. You have been in your current physical form only a short time. You are deeply in love with your divine complement. All of that gives you the potential to be a profoundly great writer."

"Why is that so?" I was hooked.

"You've accumulated few experiences that would obstruct the stories you're channeling," he explained. "The only reality you know is love – a prerequisite for writing an epic love story."

"How do you know I am narrating a love story?" I asked.

"Because a vortex of love surrounds you when you're writing," he answered.

"So I am composing a romance and not an odyssey," I asserted.

"Actually it is an odyssey," he replied. "Love is breathtaking saga. You'll know that by the end of your story. But you're only at the beginning of it."

"The beginning of the story I'm writing or the story of my life?" I queried.

"Both, for they're one and the same," he declared. Then he modified his statement. "You're writing the story of your *lives*. When you're done, you'll have foretold them all. You'll have documented every twist and turn that causes you and your love to come together, separate and unite again, over and over, until finally you merge as one, with no need ever to part."

"Must we separate in this lifetime?" I asked.

"Yes and no," was his oblique answer. "You don't need to, but you will. That's where your individual and unified choices will take you."

"If I'm writing my own story, can't I change it to make it exactly what I want?" I posed.

"Again, yes and no," he repeated. "It will be exactly as you want it, both in the story line and in your life. At times, however, you may not believe it is what you want."

"Will I remember my story in future lifetimes?" I wondered.

"You'll experience moments of recollection, when you feel that what is occurring has happened before or might occur in the future," he explained. "But in truth you'll be evoking a slice of the story as it unfolds in perfect alignment with that lifetime."

"Or perhaps as my life unfolds in perfect alignment with the story," I suggested. "Does it have a happy ending?"

"Of course," he assured me. "After all, didn't it have an auspicious beginning?"

"Most auspicious," I agreed. "Just one more question. Why should a narrative of my lives be shared? Isn't it private?"

"It is both private and universal," he answered enigmatically. "When others read your story, they will also be reading their own. Every life is a love story, and people want to find their way back to the love that defines them."

"Very well, I'll seriously consider your offer to publish my stories," I responded.

"Fair enough," he said. "I'll be back when you've decided."

"How will you know that?" I couldn't help asking.

"You'll see," he replied inscrutably before departing.

I was ambivalent about publishing the manuscript. On the one hand, I relished the freedom of allowing it to flow in any direction, with no concern for whether anyone else would find it enjoyable or plausible or even interesting. On the other hand, if others might benefit from reading it, how could I refuse?

∞ ∞ ∞

Luke arrived home that evening with a bouquet of flowers and a silk beribboned box. He was beaming.

"Looks like you had a good day," I commented, glancing from the salad I was preparing.

"I did indeed," he affirmed. "I realized that whatever is occurring at the institute, I have the most precious gift anyone could ever want. I have my true love at my side, contentedly chopping vegetables."

"Did you say contentedly?" I teased.

"It certainly appears that way," he smiled. "And so to commemorate the gift of you, I brought you a little something."

He handed me the flowers, an eclectic mix of purples, whites and vibrant spring greens. Each blossom seemed to be singing with joy and wild beauty. I arranged them in a crystal vase and set the bouquet on the dining table.

"I was thinking more in terms of the bedroom," Luke suggested.

"Ah yes, lately you've been thinking in terms of the bedroom quite often," I quipped.

"Why do you suppose?" he asked disingenuously.

"I have no idea," I replied with feigned innocence. "The patio and garden are lovely this time of year."

"Maybe I'm more interested in another garden of delights," he countered.

This banter could have gone on indefinitely. It often did. Instead he declared, "You're here, and we have each other, and I love you so much it hurts. And in the end our love will have defined my first breath of life and the last one as well."

I reached up to him, holding his face in my hands. His eyes were intense with emotion.

A terrible uncertainty descended upon me. Did I deserve such love? Could I love him as unconditionally?

"What just happened?" he asked. "A cloud came over you, more like a storm front."

"I was wondering if I am worthy of your love," I revealed.

"If I am offering it to you then you are worthy of receiving it," he whispered. "I love everything about you, even your self-doubts."

I kissed him gently. Our lips barely touched in a delicate coming together, so divinely intimate. I picked up the vase spilling over with blossoms and led the way to the bedroom.

Luke followed, carrying the tiny wooden box. I set the vase on a small round table in front of the window. It looked lovely against the mother of pearl inlays and warm cherry wood.

Luke motioned for me to sit in one of the reading chairs on either side of the table and lowered himself into the other. He placed the box beside the flowers and took my hand in his.

"We loved each other from the moment we were created, and we'll love each other until the moment we're one again," he vowed.

"In this lifetime and all others, I'll give you the ring inside this box. With this ring I pledge my eternal love. It is and ever will be. I am yours until I am you and we are one."

He handed me the box. It was made of carved sandalwood and decorated with sacred geometries. Two ribbons of iridescent gold and platinum silk were tied around it. I untied the bow and held the box in my hand, studying its design in detail. The box alone was gift enough, but I knew it contained something even more precious. I opened the lid carefully. Inside was the ring, nestled in amethyst velvet.

Two bands of gold and platinum intertwined. Each one was carved with sacred letters embedded in finely engraved geometries. The box and the ring belonged together, just like the two strands of the ring.

"This ring is incredible!" I exclaimed. "It has such artistry and spiritual power, I can't imagine what it took to create it."

"All it took was my envisioning it," Luke declared.

"You imagined it, then it simply appeared?" I asked, incredulous.

"Well, almost," he revealed. "I dreamed of the ring last night after we made love. I was searching for a ring that represented my love for you, but nothing I saw even came close. Then I stopped by a river. As I gazed at the current, the ring in the box appeared to me. I awoke with a start and willed myself to remember every detail."

"But that was just last night," I noted, wondering how the ring could have been made to his specifications in just one day.

"On my way to work this morning, I passed a blind man sitting by the road with a few trinkets to sell," Luke recounted. "I was in a hurry and almost walked by him, but a dusty old container caught my eye. I approached him and asked if I could take a closer look at it. He nodded absentmindedly. The moment I picked it up, I realized it was the box I saw in my dream. Cautiously I opened the lid, and there was the ring I dreamed into existence."

"How could you afford this gift?" I asked. "It is priceless."

"I told him I wanted to purchase both, but I had very little to pay him," Luke continued. "I handed him the box, then described it and the ring to be certain he understood their value. He inquired why they intrigued me, and I revealed that I had seen them in a dream. I said the ring was for my true love, my divine complement."

"What happened then?" I asked anxiously.

"He said with the simplicity of a sage, 'There are all forms of payment. Give me whatever you have, and make up the rest with your love.'"

I listened to Luke's story, holding the ring in the palm of my hand. Before my eyes the sacred letters changed shape and formed the words:

Eternal love

Eternal life

Eternal union

The ring had its own unique alchemy, its divine message. I recited the vow to Luke.

I arose from the chair and stood in front of him, the ring in my hand. "Please, my love, place this ring on my finger that we may never be parted for long and never lost from our love," I whispered.

He pulled me onto his lap, took the ring and slipped it on my finger. It fit perfectly.

"You are my most dearly beloved, and I am yours forever," he vowed.

"And I am yours," I replied softly.

Then we kissed. The rest I leave to the imagination, for it was too precious and private to be revealed.

∞ ∞ ∞

"What about the ribbons?" I asked first thing the next morning.

"The ribbons?" Luke mumbled, still half asleep.

"The ribbons tied around the box," I specified. "Where did you get them?"

"Ah, yes, the ribbons," he remembered. "After I purchased the box and ring with the little money I had, I headed off to work. A street fair was in progress, though one had never been in that location before.

"An old crone sitting alone with a basket of ribbons called out to me, 'Ladle with the box, you must add a bit of decoration to it.' I told her I had no way to pay her.

"'Never mind,' she replied, 'the ring in that box deserves an equally magnificent decoration.' How did she know about the ring?

"She pulled on the ends of two ribbons buried in the basket. One was made of such fine silk, it looked like spun gold. The other was sparkling silver so ethereal it could have been woven platinum.

"'You must have these,' she said, holding out her hand to receive the box. I hesitated for a moment before giving it to her, but somehow I knew she was trustworthy. She wound the ribbons around the box and tied a bow on top.

"'Gold and platinum, intertwined as one, create the only reality of your existence,' she observed. 'All else is illusion. Love all, love always, and you will never experience the unwinding of the gold and platinum. Keep your love whole, and the ring and ribbons will strengthen your bond throughout lifetimes until finally there is no gold, there is no platinum. The two will merge, as will you with your divine complement, into one glorious, infinitely expansive manifestation of love.'

"I took the beribboned box and bowed to her. 'Peace be with you,' I said in thanksgiving. 'May love light the path before you.'

"'My blessings upon you as well,' she said reverently, 'and upon your union with your true love.'

"I nodded, turned and headed toward the institute. Later that day I received an unexpected bonus. I set out for the street fair so I could share it with the ribbon vendor. In the spot where she had been was a young girl selling flowers fresh from the fields.

"'Have you seen a ribbon vendor?' I asked hopefully.

"'No, and I've been here all day,' she replied.

"'I talked with her this morning at the street fair,' I explained.

"'What street fair?' she wondered. 'There was no street fair today.'

"'No vendors lining the pathway selling their wares?' I queried.

"'None whatsoever,' she confirmed.

"She was speaking her truth. My reality, on the other hand, was quite different. I fingered the ribbon and stared absently at the flowers. Had the ribbon vendor met me in another dimension, and if so, how could two actual ribbons be tied around the box? Beyond that, where and how did I meet the old man?

"'I'm about to leave,' the flower girl said, 'and I have one bouquet left. It's my favorite, but no one wanted it. I can see it on a round table of cherry wood, with inlays intricately forming a circle. The wild irrepressibility of the flowers would enhance such an elegant piece of furniture, don't you think?'

"'Yes, they'd be beautiful together,' I agreed.

"'And you have such a table in your house?' she asked, although it was really a statement.

"'I do,' I affirmed.

"'In the bedroom?' Another statement posing as a question.

"'Yes,' I confirmed.

"'Then these flowers must go home with you,' she insisted, thrusting them into my hand.

"'How much do they cost?' I asked, preparing to pay her.

"'Nothing,' she stated flatly. 'They were talking to me this morning, telling me exactly which blossoms belonged in the bouquet and precisely where they should be placed in your home. There's just one more qualification. Do you have a crystal vase?'

"'We do,' I affirmed.

"'Then they most definitely will go home with you, a gift from Mother Nature in celebration of eternal love,' she said. 'I can't charge you for them, since I neither created nor selected them. They're not mine to sell. I'm simply a servant honoring a request.'

"'And serve is what you do exceptionally well,' I told her."

Thus Luke concluded his story.

"Extraordinary!" I exclaimed. "My understanding of what is real and what is illusion is shifting rapidly. It's as if we are living in multiple dimensions at once."

"Perhaps we are," Luke replied.

"One final question: What about the carvings on the box?" I asked.

"At the institute I researched the meaning of the sacred geometries," Luke replied. "The box features three primary shapes: the pyramid, the six-pointed star and the Merkabah. Each one is made up of triangles in different configurations.

"The pyramid consists of four equilateral triangles arranged around a square base and forming an apex at the top. It symbolizes the evolution of the human spirit. It begins at the base, fully grounded in earthly existence. The vibrational frequencies increase as one ascends the pyramid. Near the apex the vibrations are so strong, one must set aside all attachments and surrender to Source. The apex enables the complete integration of spirit into one's life in the material world.

"So the pyramid represents the path a spirit takes during human embodiment, lifetime after lifetime, until it merges again with its Creator," I summarized. "What about the other geometries?"

"The six-pointed star and the Merkabah are different representations of the same concept, except that the star is two-dimensional and the Merkabah is three-dimensional," he explained. "The six-pointed star represents the perfect balance of the masculine and feminine, one triangle being the masculine principle and the other being the feminine. This symbolizes the potential to create harmony, complementarity and sustainability. It also represents physical union. The triangle pointing downward is the male, penetrating the female.

"The Merkabah is emblematic of spiritual union. Whereas the six-pointed, two-dimensional star epitomizes perfect balance between complementary opposites, the Merkabah symbolizes their ultimate merging. When they unite as one the Merkabah spins in all directions, creating a sphere of light. This return of two to oneness is catalytic, setting the Merkabah in motion so they are never separated again.

"The box tells our story and the ring confirms our togetherness – gold and platinum – as long as we continue to be born on Earth," I said in benediction. "Which one of us is gold and which one is platinum?"

"I wondered the same thing," Luke responded. "Then I recalled you sitting in the sun, a halo of spun gold around your head. You're my golden girl."

∞ ∞ ∞

"I witnessed something at work today that proved my concerns haven't been unfounded," Luke disclosed a few weeks later. "I was allowed inside the dormitory for the people involved in experiments. Their beds are barely two feet apart. It looked like a factory, not a residence. No one in their right mind could live under such circumstances."

"Maybe they're not in their right minds," I suggested.

"I don't think they are," he continued. "In fact, I doubt their minds are functioning at all. When I see them walking around the compound, it's as if I am watching robots. Previously they were multi-faceted human beings. Now they're only shells, more dead than alive. They've lost the spark of spirit, and their brains can't function independently."

"Is something or someone controlling their minds?" I asked.

"That I don't know," he replied. "They've lost their connection with humanity, either because it was programmed out of them or because it's being manipulated by a source of external control. Perhaps both."

"It sounds diabolical," I said warily.

"Maybe, maybe not," he cautioned. "Perhaps an experiment involving a large number of people accidentally went wrong, and this is the result. On the other hand, a premeditated decision might have been made to involve human beings in an experiment that causes them to lose their mental, emotional and spiritual capacities. If so, it must be stopped."

"Don't speak of this to anyone at the institute," I urged. "Avoid causing any of your colleagues to believe you are concerned or even curious. Appear to be oblivious and unobservant. When people relax around you, they may reveal their secrets. Over time you might learn all you need to know. Then you can decide on the most appropriate course of action."

"Wise advice from someone who writes adventure stories," he quipped.

"No one said adventuresses aren't also strategic!" I replied.

I was in the dunes, engrossed in a new story line, when a familiar shadow appeared on the page. I looked up and saw Julian standing before me, his silhouette illuminated by the sun. The glow around his head seemed more radiant than ever.

"How are the lovers doing?" he asked cheerfully.

"Very much in love with love and loving each other," I replied brightly.

"Excellent!" he exclaimed. "May that always be the case, whatever travails befall them."

"Who said there are any travails?" I asked, wondering how he knew.

"They are living on the Earth plane, where it is the exception to avoid travails," he observed.

"I suppose so," I assented. "But a challenge every now and then can make love grow stronger."

"In the context of your story, I'd agree," he replied. "Your love would only deepen in the face of an assault. But not all love can withstand trials, or even minor skirmishes. Lesser love blows with the wind, bringing happiness during good times and disillusionment during difficult ones. Your love remains steadfast, whatever the circumstances."

"It may be a love story for all time," I noted, "but I wonder whether it's a love story for all people."

"Precisely," he agreed. His comment surprised me. I'd expected him to argue the opposite. "Let's say the average person, if there is such a being, experiences love as something fragile or perhaps even unattainable. Maybe it's unrequited. What possible benefit would a story about true love's holding steady through threats of change and destruction, have for such a person?"

"It would offer a ray of hope that love is possible," I noted. "Even more fundamentally, love is what binds us to each other and to our Creator. The spark of spirit within us is pure love. Whatever enhances that love is a gift. If a story can do that every now and then, all the better."

"You convinced me!" he exclaimed, chuckling. Then I realized he had turned the tables on my hesitation and led me to make my own arguments in favor of publishing my writings. I didn't know whether to complain or congratulate him on his tactics of persuasion.

"If you're half as good at selling your publications as you are at convincing budding authors to turn their manuscripts over to you, you must be wildly successful," I commented.

"I'm successful, maybe even wildly so," he admitted, "but not because of any particular skill. I simply recognize those whose work is worthy of being made available to others. The rest takes care of itself."

"And you believe my writing is worthy, though you haven't read a word of it?" I challenged.

"We've been here before," he reminded me. "I can read *you*, which is more important than reading your manuscripts. I can tell by the vibrations you radiate when you're absorbed in your writing that your story would be a divinely inspired gift to all."

And with that he was gone.

One, Beyond Time

PART TWO
ANNA AND JESSE

My life is blessed. Love and peace surround me.

Little effort goes into what I do, though I accomplish a great deal by the end of each day. The pages in my journal, which were blank just a few hours earlier, are filled with new revelations in an unfolding story. That is remarkable even to me, perhaps especially to me.

I've also been spending mornings in the garden cultivating herbs, vegetables and aromatic plants. Pots of lavender, rosemary and sage infuse our home with subtle fragrances. I tend the plants with affection, and they offer me their stems and branches, blossoms and roots in return.

Each plant has its own personality and voice. The plants speak to me, never hesitating to reveal their purpose and preferences. I follow their advice assiduously.

When destructive insects attack the roses, the blossoms tell me how to purge them. The herbs, on the other hand, emphasize their unique healing properties. I experiment with them to alleviate minor ailments. Lately I've been using them more for that purpose than to enhance the flavor of roasts and stews.

Once when I was about to make a marinade with ground herbs and peppers, they proposed, "Create a bouquet instead to simmer in the broth." The flavor was sublime.

Communing with my garden is a new ritual I follow before I select what to cook. Instead of wondering, "What shall I prepare today?" I quiz the plants: "Which of you wants to grace our table and our palate?" Inevitably I hear a chorus of volunteers.

At first I doubted whether the eclectic combination of flavors the plants themselves suggested could possibly work together. I used my own supposedly better judgment, omitting or adding ingredients, and something would be a bit off. Finally I surrendered to the plants' own culinary guidance. They knew how to blend their distinct qualities. After all, they'd grown up together.

Whenever Luke and I were invited to meals at our neighbors' homes, I took something I created at the behest of the garden itself. People would ask me where I got the recipe, and I'd reply, "I simply picked what was ripe in the garden and made it up from there."

The dinner guests would nod approvingly and acknowledge my clever talents.

One morning when I was pulling weeds my neighbor came to the gate. "I'm relieved to find you here," she said. "Fortuna has a fever, and she keeps insisting the only thing that will help her get better is a bowl of your soup. Do you have any leftovers?"

"I have no soup right now, but I'd be happy to make some for her," I replied. "Give me a couple of hours, and I'll bring it to your house. Meanwhile, tell Fortuna I know exactly what she needs. She'll be feeling fine in no time."

My neighbor smiled and thanked me. No doubt she thought if Fortuna recovered quickly, it would be due more to the power of positive thinking than my soup.

The plants indicated which herbs would cleanse and strengthen Fortuna's immune system: elderflower, yarrow and licorice root. I added them to potatoes, leeks and broth, asking every ingredient to sweep away her fever.

When the soup was perfectly blended, I took the pot to my neighbor's house. She ladled a small amount into a bowl, and we took it into Fortuna's room.

"Is that my soup?" she asked hopefully. "I saw you making it in the kitchen."

Her mother hastened to explain to me, "Fortuna has an active imagination. She's constantly saying she saw something when she wasn't even there." I decided not to challenge her explanation, though I was well aware Fortuna had "seen" me in a different way.

"Eat up, dear one," I told her, "and soon you'll be good as new."

She devoured the soup and asked, "Could I have more, only this time would you fill the bowl to the top?"

After Fortuna consumed the second more generous helping, her fever subsided.

"I feel lots better already, Mama," she reported, "all because of Grace's soup."

"Nonetheless, stay in bed the rest of the day," I suggested. "Tomorrow you can play outside."

"Okay," she agreed, "but only if you promise to make soup for me whenever I'm sick."

"And even when you are not," I assured her.

That evening Luke arrived home so distraught, I was sorry I hadn't made a double batch of that healing mélange.

"I found more evidence of wrongdoing at work today," he revealed. "After we completed an experiment, I was entering the results in our database. I sat behind a one-way window and couldn't be seen from the observation room.

"The door burst open, and two institute directors rushed in. They closed the door behind them and looked around to be sure no one was there. I remained completely still so as not to betray my presence in the other room.

"One of the men began shouting at the other one. 'How could you have been so careless? You knew the inspectors were coming this morning, and all evidence of mental illness resulting from the experiments was to be erased from the files.'

"The other man responded, 'I had no idea our records would be so thoroughly analyzed. No one has ever done that before. I told you we never should have reported problematic results in the first place. Any trail leading to information about what we're really doing would be disastrous.'

"The first man replied, 'I know, but we have to account for everyone involved. It would raise too much suspicion if half the subjects in our experiments vanished from our files. Tell me, what did the inspectors find?'

"'Nothing as far as I can determine,' the other reported, 'but I overheard someone saying the files don't make sense. One of the investigators dug deep enough to realize we might have falsified the data.'

"'Falsified in some instances, but not all of them,' corrected the first man. 'Much of the data is accurate. We doctored it only after we identified the side effects of our more extreme experiments on mind manipulation.'

"'We should lay low for a while in case there is a follow-up investigation. The underling who uncovered the discrepancies has little credibility. I plan to discredit his work so he'll be transferred before the next inspection. In the meantime, we have to do something about those files.'

"'What do you suggest? We can't create a technological malfunction, because we might lose all the archives in the process,' the first man warned. 'We're too far along to risk it. With more time, we may have a breakthrough that enables us to control the brain functioning of the masses. All we need to do now is make sure that overzealous twit doesn't come around here again. I'll take care of that.'

"'Okay, you're the boss,' the second man agreed, and that was the end of it."

"They never realized you were overhearing their conversation?" I verified.

"They had no idea anyone was within shouting distance," Luke assured me. "I waited quite a while before I left, so as not to arouse any suspicion."

"Do you know which records they were talking about?" I asked.

"Yes and no," he responded. "I have access to the system in order to enter results from the experiments I'm monitoring. But I'm working only with the database that records more beneficial conclusions. I haven't witnessed destructive experiments, nor have I seen documentation describing their impact on the people subjected to them."

"Even so, you now have clear evidence of wrongdoing, which you've suspected for some time," I noted.

"I can't allow people to be damaged without trying to stop it," he declared. "I intend to find out everything I can without drawing attention to myself. If this is a false alarm, and I hope it is, I can rest easier. If it is not, we'll decide what I should do."

"You just said *we* would decide," I noted.

"Yes, I said *we* and I meant it," he affirmed. "If I am to step into the fray, it will be our decision, not mine alone. I'd never take the risk of exposing abuses unless you agree there is no other alternative."

"A shared responsibility would be easier for each of us to bear," I admitted.

"We share everything," he whispered. "Significant decisions will always be mutual."

∞ ∞ ∞

A theme playing out in my writing was at once fascinating and disconcerting. The female protagonist was beginning to develop her own character and competencies. In so doing, she was gradually differentiating herself from her lover. I used the term "differentiating" and not "distancing," for as she became more herself, she met her lover in the context of his own growing complexity. They were becoming more individual but not more separate, more independent and yet also more interdependent.

I recalled when we left the temples and first came to our house. Because we were so unfamiliar with how to live as man and woman, we approached the world together. As Luke's complement, I was aware of how he thought, felt and perceived.

I loved everything about Luke, not because I fantasized him as my protector or denied my own needs for the sake of our relationship. Rather, I loved him because I saw exactly who he was and loved exactly who he was and related to all those qualities effortlessly.

We began as identical people, our only difference being gender. But as time progressed, we started to follow paths that delineated us more distinctly as individuals. He chose to be the one earning the resources we needed, and I took up writing. He went into the community every day, and I tended my garden and listened to the herbs tell me of their healing powers.

Luke was incapable of looking the other way if someone was treated with disrespect or if an act of trust was dishonored. He carried the world on his shoulders, and I was a free spirit who loved her solitude. Whereas he was intent on righting blatant wrongs, my life was more interior. He focused on realigning from the outside in, and I worked from the inside out.

As I said, we became differentiated beyond gender.

Whereas he brought his experiences to our conversations, I contributed my private adventures. Each of us was intrigued by what the other was doing and becoming. Rather than pulling us apart, our emerging individuality strengthened our bond.

We grew together not because we remained exactly as we were in the beginning, but because we embraced opportunities to learn, expand and change. There was nothing static about either our independence or our togetherness. The more he became Luke and I became Grace, the more we had to offer one another. As we grew more idiosyncratic, our relationship developed new facets that made it ever more compelling.

And so we loved. Days became weeks and months and then one year.

Gardening and healing gradually replaced my writing. The soup I made for Fortuna launched me unexpectedly onto a new trajectory.

I was developing a reputation as a natural healer. As more and more people requested consultations with me, I created an expanding array of potions and powders, oils and creams. I was rapidly running out of space to do this work well.

Every last area outside was devoted to growing herbs and healing plants. Our spare room was filled with herbs in containers and flowers drying in bunches.

The kitchen became overwhelmed with ingredients for my healing ministrations.

One morning Luke and I were relaxing outside, an increasingly rare moment, when he suggested, "Why don't you find another location where you can practice your healing arts? You'd have the room you need, and we could get our house back."

"I'm not a trained healer," I protested. "If I set up shop elsewhere, people may assume I'm more capable than I actually am."

"Is anyone asking about your credentials?" he questioned.

"No one has brought it up," I responded. "People believe I can help them, and quite honestly I usually do."

"Now that you've made your own case," Luke chuckled, "let's find an office that suits you."

There was a particular twinkle in his eyes, one I had seen before when he was fairly bursting with a surprise for me.

"I have a better idea," I chirped. "Why don't we go directly to the space you've already located?"

"It's impossible to surprise you," he laughed.

"Not impossible," I corrected him. "I'm always surprised when you surprise yourself."

We walked into town. On the main avenue by the ocean was an unassuming one-story building with a For Rent sign. Before I even peered in the windows, I knew it was mine.

A few minutes later, by design as it turned out, the landlord arrived and showed us around. The space included a waiting room, two consultation rooms and a large area for storing and mixing herbs. The rooms opened onto each other, creating flexible space enhanced by fresh ocean breezes.

"We'll take it!" I exclaimed before I even knew the price. Luke smiled in satisfaction.

I spent the next month preparing to open my health and healing center. Paint in soothing ocean tones transformed the drab interior. Furniture cushions and accessories ranging in color from aquamarine to cream and pale gold enhanced the calming effect. I placed pots of plants, herbs and flowers inside and out, along with crystals, rocks and shells of all sorts.

Aware I couldn't do everything by myself, I hired two people to assist me. I chose them for their happy spirits and generous hearts. Although I hadn't yet defined their responsibilities, I was confident that would soon be clear. All I had left to do was hope we could help enough people to stay in business.

That wasn't a problem. Word that I had opened a healing center spread quickly. Within a few months I added a third staff person. The center was thriving, as were the people who came to see us.

My writing continued, but only infrequently. Every now and then I paused from my work to sit on the deck overlooking the water, open myself to spirit and fill a few journal pages. I found my calling as a healer, but I also enjoyed the inspiration of writing. With both available to me, the days passed in ever more meaningful ways.

Luke spent months secretly documenting what transpired at the institute, both recently and over the course of decades. He uncovered a web so complicated it's a wonder anyone escaped unscathed from the experiments. We frequently discussed the abuses he was discovering and more importantly, what he should do about them.

It was both puzzling and disconcerting that no one previously came forth with evidence similar to what Luke unearthed. He was no detective, and he'd worked at the institute only a short time. Yet he gathered unassailable proof of systematic wrongdoing. Why hadn't others with more experience and knowledge done so already?

I feared the situation was more treacherous than either of us dared admit. I even rued the day he overheard the damning conversation that thrust him onto this hazardous path. If he publicly revealed what he knew, the backlash against him would doubtless be swift and severe.

"I must ask you one more time," I commented one evening. "Are you certain high ranking people at the institute knowingly jeopardize the mental and physical health of others in conducting their experiments?"

"Beyond a shadow of a doubt," Luke confirmed.

"How can they get away with it?" I wondered.

"The institute advertises for volunteers willing to be paid a significant sum in exchange for signing away their independence," he explained. "They must meet many requirements, not the least of which is that they have no living family or next of kin."

"Why is that?" I asked.

"The institute doesn't want to involve people with close ties to the outside world," Luke explained. "Loners are best, as are those who believe a confined life is preferable to the one they've been leading. However, there is a more diabolical reason for selecting people abandoned by circumstance or choice: If they never reappear, no one will come looking for them."

"Do these people realize they may never leave the institute?" I continued.

"Initially they are told they can opt out at any time," Luke replied. "But soon they're separated from their capacity to think independently."

"How can that happen?" I asked.

"Early in the process a microchip is implanted in their brain during what appears to be a routine physical examination," Luke revealed. "The implant is tiny – virtually invisible – but it can influence and even control the person's every thought, emotion and action. Once the implant has been successfully embedded, all notions of leaving the institute disappear. The implant reads unwanted thought forms and neutralizes them immediately.

"It works the other way as well. The implant receives transmissions from external sources and sends them into the brain as if the idea had derived from the person's own thought process. What people perceive to be their normal brain functioning is actually something they receive from elsewhere. It's unimaginably corrupt.

"They're subjected to control over their thoughts, emotions, beliefs and attitudes, after which they are closely observed. Behavior change is measured, as are physiological shifts such as heartbeat, blood pressure and brain waves. The most nuanced differences are tracked."

"But the overall impact of these experiments isn't nuanced at all!" I exclaimed.

"Indeed," Luke nodded. "I have no idea how many people have been essentially annihilated over the years. My guess is that once participants in the experiments are lost completely, they are permanently relocated to a facility where they get little care and are treated no better than animals."

"Maybe worse than animals," I conjectured.

"Probably so," Luke agreed.

"What causes some people to lose touch with who they are and others to exhibit few ill effects?" I asked.

"It all depends on which group they are assigned to," Luke observed. "This isn't a random process. Comprehensive analyses are done on each person's genetics, background, intelligence, personality, physical characteristics, health, psychology and other factors. Based on the findings, a recommendation is then made regarding which group each individual will join."

"How many experiments are being conducted?" I inquired.

"Thousands were done over the years, and new ones are being developed all the time," Luke revealed. "There's a never ending stream of hypotheses to be tested and questions to be answered. Comprehensive records are kept on each experiment, along with measurable short- and long-term effects."

"Why has no one put the pieces together?" I persisted.

"Good question. The people running the institute are proud of their leading edge work and keep meticulous records," Luke noted. "But they cover their tracks by documenting each experiment separately. It's impossible to cull through massive records and make definitive connections among them.

"I have a hunch, however, that another database exists to which only select people have access – one that enables experiments to be collated and compared. It might also contain extensive documentation of experimental results over time.

"I intend to earn the trust of those in charge until I'm admitted to their inner sanctum. Then I'll suggest I might be able to determine what they're looking for by analyzing longitudinal data.

"I've been engaged only in positive, life affirming experimentation that enhances people's self worth, mental health and spiritual unfolding. No computer inputs are being used with my group. I'll be comparing them with another group receiving neurological inputs designed to support their spiritual emergence. Some researchers hope the computer can control the spirit the same way it does the mind. I'll prove the power of spirit is greater than anything technology can do to inspire, or destroy, that spark."

"You believe those in touch with their own divinity and guided by spirit would achieve a higher level of inner peace than those receiving external transmissions," I summarized. "But even if you prove this, how would it change things?"

"The people running the institute are fascinated with power," Luke explained. "They study every aspect of human consciousness to define the ultimate source of influence. But they've missed the point. No artificial manipulation comes close to the strength of one's own divinity. Nothing can control or overpower the human spirit."

∞ ∞ ∞

I haven't mentioned that a child was on the way, simply because there was none. It was not for our lack of lovemaking, which we enjoyed with a combination of familiarity and intimacy, passion and tenderness. We did nothing to prevent conception, for we acutely wanted a child. The herbs I used to enhance my fertility had no effect, although many women who came to me for such assistance conceived soon after they started taking them.

I don't recall precisely when I knew I was incapable of becoming pregnant. Perhaps it was during a walk on the beach, or while I was tending my garden, or when Luke's seed was within me and yet again no child would result from our union.

At first I told myself we just needed more time. But as additional cycles of the moon waxed and waned and I remained barren, my certainty increased. One evening in the living room I commented, "I don't think I am capable of bearing children."

"How can you be so sure?" Luke asked.

"I listen to my body the same way I hear my plants and herbs," I noted. "And I'm being told I can't conceive."

"Should you give up so easily?" Luke pressed. "Technologies are available to make the necessary repairs and realignments, with no discomfort or side effects. Whatever needs adjustment may be easy to correct."

"I considered that," I acknowledged. "And every time I thought about undergoing such intervention, be it laser surgery or hormonal stimulation, it was unacceptable to me. I don't want my body to come into contact with a foreign frequency."

"That may not be necessary," Luke observed. "A simpler solution might be available."

"For now, let's allow Mother Nature to guide the way and enjoy ourselves in the process," I suggested.

"Come here," whispered Luke, "so I can wrap you in my arms and never let you go."

Luke was sprawled on the chaise. I leaned over him, replying, "Well, then, open those generous arms of yours and let me in." I snuggled into him, arranged a soft blanket over us, and was soon fast asleep.

Sometime in the night Luke carried me to bed. I remembered being undressed and tucked in with his inimitable tenderness. He slipped in behind me and settled his long frame against mine, then whispered something I'll never forget: "Whether it is in the stars to have a family, we have each other. And that's more than enough. Sleep well, my love."

That night I dreamed I was giving birth to dozens of babies, each one belonging to a different family. I brought a child into the world, and then his or her parents stopped by to pick up their new boy or girl. As the dream progressed, I became a midwife, helping women give birth. The children I thought were mine were actually the offspring of others. Our connection, the sisterhood among women, ran deep.

That dream stayed with me throughout my life. I have assisted with hundreds of births, and not a single mother or child has been lost. The arrival of new life is a miracle. No matter how many times I experience the wonder of it, I offer up a prayer of gratitude to our Creator.

I underwent more tests than I care to recount. Each one resulted in the proposal of more extreme measures guaranteed to enhance my fertility, all of which I declined. Eventually Luke and I accepted that our biological family wouldn't grow beyond the two of us.

I was more comfortable with that prospect than he was. I spent my days with mothers and newborns, children and elderly people who received the benefits of herbal compounds and other wellness measures. I didn't experience a void in my life, since children were in and out all day.

Exuding equanimity, Luke voiced no regret. Instead he reminded me of how much he loved me, and how our love was more than enough.

∞   ∞   ∞

I am fully aware of how this narrative is bumping along in fits and starts. There are no segues to create smooth, effortless transitions. I speak with my own voice, making no attempt to sound like an autobiographer or even a fiction writer. I expect anyone who might somehow read this to saunter along with me, as if we were friends meeting for tea and resuming where we left off before, even though a great deal might have happened in between. I considered changing the style and decided against it. This is how the story wants to be told.

One afternoon I tucked myself away in the dunes and began writing fluidly. I was in the middle of a particularly exciting passage, engrossed in the unfolding adventure and oblivious to anyone or anything around me. Only the tale existed.

A familiar shadow appeared across the page. It was Julian. I didn't know whether to scold him for causing me to lose my train of thought or to welcome his inevitable observations. I chose the latter.

"Look who turned up on this gorgeous day," I exclaimed.

"It is I who should be making that observation," he replied. "You haven't been writing lately, but you are a welcome sight today. I can tell by your aura you are having no difficulty getting back into the groove."

"None at all," I affirmed.

"Are you still captivated by the saga you are recounting?" he asked.

"If I weren't, would you see me here today?" I quipped.

"I suppose not," he chuckled. "I'm wondering if you're ready to show your work to me. I'd be honored to read anything you have written so far, not to criticize it but to assuage my curiosity."

"Here is how I suggest we proceed," I began. "You may read the material in my presence. Promise to speak to no one about the stories and let me decide whether to make them public. Finally, if they are published, I want no connection with them."

"What you require is only appropriate," he responded. "When the time is right we can arrange for me to read what is pouring through you. Until then peace be with you."

"And with you," I responded.

I never saw Julian again.

I understand now that his purpose was never to publish my narratives. Rather, it was to affirm their validity and strengthen my motivation to continue. On that particular afternoon, however, he appeared for a different reason – to interrupt the flow of the story. I was unable to continue writing after he left.

Deciding to head home early, I took the long way around. The golden rays of autumn enhanced everything I glimpsed, which glowed like subtle candlelight.

I was about to turn onto the path leading to the house when I saw a child sitting alone on the ground, playing with a few small rocks. She was young, no older than five years of age, and surprisingly unafraid given that she was by herself.

I looked around for an adult or older child accompanying her. Finding no one in sight, I decided to wait with her until someone responsible for her arrived.

"Hello," I greeted her. "Do you live around here?"

I was sure she didn't, since I had never seen her before. Beyond that, the sandals and plain white shift she wore weren't what anyone I knew would put on a child.

"No, I'm not from here," she said simply.

"Are you waiting for someone?" I asked casually.

"Not really. I came by myself," she stated matter-of-factly.

"Where from?" I pressed.

"I came from a big crystal, after an explosion," she revealed. "They took me to a place with all women and girls. But I missed my brother and sneaked away so I could find him."

I was alarmed at this disclosure. She was too young to have been involved in a split, yet she described essentially what Luke and I experienced.

"When did you sneak away?" I asked.

"Yesterday," she replied.

"Where did you sleep last night?" I continued.

"In the dunes," she said. "I stayed warm there, away from the wind off the ocean."

"Have you eaten today?" I questioned.

"No," she admitted. "I'm really hungry."

"Would you like to come home with me for a bite to eat?" I asked expectantly. "I don't live far from here."

"Okay," she said, standing up and reaching for my hand.

When we got to the house I offered her bread and honey while I prepared our meal. She was comfortable and surprisingly self-possessed.

"Tell me about your brother," I suggested, angling for more information.

"I first saw him when we were standing next to each other in the big crystal with the points," she disclosed. "Before that I remember an explosion of light. I was really scared. Then I went somewhere else. When I came back into the crystal my brother was there. He was the same as me, only a boy."

As I suspected this young thing had gone through a split, even though the procedure was supposedly not available to children. One had to be an adult to make such a life-altering decision.

"I screamed and yelled and bit people when they pulled us apart. I didn't want to go anywhere without him," she explained. "But they dragged me away and told me I'd be happy where I was going. I wasn't. I cried and cried. At night I would go to sleep and fly away to meet him. Then when I woke up and saw he was gone, I cried again."

"Of course you were very sad," I said with genuine empathy. "Did anyone help you? Were the women where you lived nice to you?"

"No, they told me to stop crying and forget about ever seeing my brother again," she revealed. "Then yesterday when we were allowed outside to play, I escaped. I ran fast to get far away and ended up at the ocean. Now I have to find my brother."

She was gutsy and more determined than any other five-year-old I had encountered. Actually, she reminded me of Luke when he came for me insisting he couldn't survive without me. She could have been his daughter.

"What's your name?" I asked gently.

"I don't have one," she replied.

They hadn't even bothered to give the girl a name after she arrived. "Well, now you can pick one you like," I offered. "Do you know what it might be?"

"Anna," she said definitively.

"Then Anna it is," I declared. "Tell me, why did you select that name?"

"Because Anna was the nicest lady where I used to live," she explained. "She would hug me and tell me she knew how I felt. She said she missed her brother too."

"Don't worry, Anna," I said softly. "We'll find your brother. But first, we must take care of you."

When Luke arrived home that evening, he saw I was not alone. Assuming a neighbor or a patient from my healing center had dropped off the child in an emergency, he took it all in stride.

"Hello," he said to Anna. "Have you had a good day?"

"I've had a very good day," she chirped.

"And what made it so very good?" he pursued.

"I started out looking for my brother," she replied. "I haven't found him yet. But Grace brought me here, and I had a delicious meal and a nap. Then she gave me paints and I made a picture."

"Sounds like a very good day indeed," Luke affirmed, looking quizzically at me.

I intervened. "I discovered Anna on my way home from the beach. She was alone, so I asked her if I could help. She told me about her brother, whom she saw for the first time in an object made of crystal that had big points."

I looked squarely at Luke. He understood what I was signaling to him. I could read his thoughts: "She's too young to have been split into two by choice.

Someone must have done it by force. This is an outrage."

I nodded wordlessly, and he blinked in complicity.

"Anna was taken away from her brother, but she escaped so she could look for him," I explained.

"Do you know where your brother is?" Luke asked.

"No," she replied. "We meet every night while we are sleeping, when we fly in the sky. I don't know where he goes when he wakes up."

"We'll find him," Luke assured her. "Meanwhile, you can stay with us if you want."

"I'd like that," Anna answered immediately. "Your house is a lot nicer than where I was before. Can my brother come here too? He's the only family I have."

"We're not exactly your family," I said soothingly. "But we'll treat you as if we were. And we'll search for your brother."

Anna began weeping with relief, rubbing her eyes with her tiny fists. Luke picked her up with the sweep of his arm and settled her on his lap. Feeling secure, finally, she gave herself over to a flood of tears. Luke rocked her and told her not to worry, that everything would be all right. I left him to comfort her while I prepared dinner.

When the meal was ready, they were fast asleep in the living room. Anna was snuggled on Luke's lap like a kitten, and he was holding her so securely, even in his sleep she was in no danger of going anywhere.

I leaned against a pillar and contemplated how our lives had changed since the day had dawned. Luke's ease and loving care toward Anna affirmed that already she was part of our family.

Nonetheless, she wasn't supposed to be with us. If people began asking around, it wouldn't take them long to discover that a five-year-old girl with a tousled mane of copper curls and determined green eyes was inexplicably part of our household. Any day someone might come knocking on our door to retrieve her.

What rights did we have? No doubt a governmental institution had already laid claim to Anna and was planning to force her back into custody when she was located. If we presented ourselves as her potential guardians, we would be required to turn her over to those who housed her initially.

Then there was the question of the boy Anna called her brother. We must find a way to bring them together safely and live with us.

Luke stirred and opened his eyes with a start. For a moment he had no recollection of who the little girl asleep in his lap might be. Then he smiled softly and kissed Anna on the top of her head.

I motioned for Luke to follow me, and he carried her into the spare bedroom where a sleeping cot was ready for her. He laid her down gently and tucked her under the covers. We left a candle burning and the door slightly ajar so she would feel safe in unfamiliar surroundings.

Over dinner Luke and I discussed what to do. "I don't want to take her back to wherever she came from, yet I wonder if she can stay here without being discovered," I noted. "Plus, she wants to be with the boy. How will we ever rescue him?"

"Why do you think he, or she for that matter, needs to be rescued?" Luke asked, more to learn what I had been thinking than to challenge my assertion.

"For one simple reason," I replied. "No five-year-old understands the implications of the split she experienced. It had to have been decided for them by someone in authority. And given that they ended up in a communal setting instead of a family, I doubt the people who arranged the split had positive purposes in mind."

"Anna couldn't have made up the story about the Merkabah," Luke asserted. "Even if she overheard others talking about it, she wouldn't have recounted the experience so precisely. She described exactly what happened to us. Most persuasive, though, is her desperate need to find her twin. I understand that. Let's keep Anna here while we consider what to do. Meanwhile, I'll try to find out where she was before."

"If all goes well, would you consider having her live with us permanently?" I asked hesitantly.

"I would," Luke declared.

"And her twin?" I continued.

"It goes without saying, wherever she is, he must be as well," Luke replied decisively.

We went to bed and talked at length about how we could keep Anna safe until Luke acquired more information. Uncharacteristically, we made detailed plans. We didn't want to take any chance she would be seen and identified as the runaway girl.

Luke kissed me softly and whispered, "Maybe we can't have children of our own because all along we were meant to raise Anna and her twin. I hope that is so, because she has already found her way into my heart."

"Mine too," I murmured, "which is what worries me. I couldn't bear to see her returned to the people who had her first."

"Then we'll make sure that doesn't happen," Luke affirmed.

We made love that night, slowly at first so we could caress each other in all the places that gave us the most pleasure. Our lovemaking was natural and effortless. We took our time touching, kissing and stimulating one another in a seductively meandering way.

Our love existed in the context of a new reality: Luke and I had each other and a family. I knew with every facet of my being that Anna and her brother would be our children.

A few hours later Luke nudged me awake. "Have any of the women who come to you for healing told you they were aware when life was created?" he inquired.

I pulled myself out of the cloud of sleep. "Some women knew when they conceived," I replied. "It was more an innate recognition than a physical sensation."

"And did you feel that way tonight when we made love?" Luke asked, pulling me to him.

"I did," I replied, "even though there is no life within me."

"But there is life with us," he responded. "She sleeps in the other room, and he sleeps somewhere yet to be determined."

I brought my body alongside his. Kissing him softly I said, "At long last you are about to become a father."

∞ ∞ ∞

The next day I took Anna to buy new clothes so she could blend in with other children in the community. Before we left home I pulled her hair back and tied a scarf around her head. Her copper curls were too distinguishing a characteristic to leave uncovered. By crisscrossing another scarf at her midriff and tying it around her waist, I disguised her stark white shift as well.

Since it was early in the day, the streets were relatively deserted. We encountered no one I knew. A few new outfits later, we walked home hand-in-hand. Her shift was hidden in a bag under our purchases. I'd dispose of it immediately.

Then an insight struck me. After Julian interrupted me the day before, I couldn't resume my writing. That was uncharacteristic. Leaving the dunes earlier than I planned, I started for home and found Anna. Julian's purpose was to make sure I left precisely when I did.

Who was he – a prophet or a publisher? I wasn't certain.

Anna interrupted my thoughts with a question. "When we find my brother, will we take him shopping for new clothes?"

"Yes we will," I assured her. "And you can help pick them out, if he's willing to let you."

"Where will he sleep?" she pursued. "You don't have any more beds."

"He can sleep on the comfy chaise until we make other arrangements," I improvised. "You can try it out to see if you think he'd like it."

"Will he be able to choose his own name as well?" she wondered.

"That depends on whether he already has one," I replied. "Someone may have given him a name, in which case he'll probably want to keep it."

"I'll ask him when I see him tonight while we sleep," she declared. "I'll also let him know we are coming to get him and he has a place to sleep and good food to eat."

"Tell him it may take a while for us to find him," I cautioned. "Ask him to be patient and remember we are trying hard to discover where he is."

"But I already know where he is!" Anna exclaimed. "He told me last night. He's at an institute."

A chill came over me. Was the research center where Luke worked somehow involved in this travesty? And if so, where were they keeping the children?

While Anna played outside, I contemplated the future. What would become of her and her twin if they were brought up as brother and sister then came to love each other as Luke and I did? No doubt the same connection we experienced united them.

When, if ever, would we tell them they weren't siblings? If we perpetuated the illusion they were born of the same mother and father, would that harm them later? As they grew into adulthood would they want to become lovers?

Anna approached me with a handful of lavender from the garden. "This is for you, for being so nice," she offered.

"And this is for you, for being just as nice," I replied, hugging her. "Let's go inside and find a lovely container for these flowers."

Arranging them in a lime green vase, I asked her, "Where do you want to place this sweet smelling bouquet?"

"By the chair where Luke and I napped last night," she responded at once.

"And why is that?" I wondered.

"Because as I was falling asleep, I smelled the lavender growing in the garden," she explained. "Then I flew to meet my brother. Guess what? He had brought me these very same flowers."

"I suggest we put them by your bed," I offered, "so that when you go to sleep tonight, the fragrance will be there for you both."

"But I gave the flowers to you," Anna protested.

"And I'm giving them to you," I smiled, "just like your brother did."

We set the vase on a table by her bed. Anna hopped on top of the bed and announced, "I'm sleepy. I think I'll take a nap." I kissed her and left her to slumber.

It was difficult to decide what to do next. Trying to write would be hopeless, and I didn't have anything essential to do around the house. I decided to tend a neglected area of the garden.

As I was trimming plants and pulling up unwanted volunteers, I had a strong sensation that something terrible was about to happen. Then I saw myself in the distant future, harvesting plants and preparing to take them with me. The garden was much larger and in a different location, but still by the sea. A man I didn't recognize was helping me. I packed the most important plants with dirt around the roots so they could survive a long journey. Others I would allow to dry and use for their healing properties as well as their seeds, which I hoped to plant in a new garden far away.

Luke was assembling essentials we would need, calling out to me to make haste. I heard him say, "The ship is sailing soon. We must be there on time. Take what you can and leave the rest." I tried to discern if Anna and the boy were with us, but I couldn't tell.

We were turning our backs on the life we had led because we had an opportunity to depart before disaster occurred.

Suddenly I was back in my garden, shaken and shaking. The fragrance of the lavender was potent in the afternoon sun. Revived, I walked beyond the rows of herbs and gazed at the ocean. Yet another vision arrived. We were sailing away from the island, moving rapidly with the wind at our backs. Anna and her brother were with us. They appeared to be in their twenties. We were saying goodbye silently, privately, to the place we called home all our lives.

The island erupted in multiple explosions. Fires burned everywhere, sending light high into the sky. Then the Earth rumbled and groaned beneath us. The ocean crested in enormous waves, threatening to engulf our boat. Just as we were about to go below deck for safety, the island was submerged in the sea.

We strapped ourselves into paneled seats in the ship's hold and prepared to ride out the chaos in the ocean, praying the boat would hold together in the turbulence.

When my consciousness returned to my body a second time, birds were chirping and the warm breeze off the ocean was blowing the tendrils of my hair. I was standing on solid ground. Although my being was quaking, the Earth was not. I went inside for a glass of water and passed out in a chair before I made it to the bedroom.

Awakening a bit later, I considered what I just experienced. If it was a portent of things to come, apparently we had a couple of decades before it occurred. My more immediate concerns, keeping Anna in our family and finding her twin, took precedence over this admittedly apocalyptic vision. I put it out of my mind.

After dinner, when Anna was asleep for the night, I told Luke that her brother was at an institute. Although a number of them were in the area, I thought he might begin by checking at the one where he worked.

"Today I casually asked a few people if they'd heard of small children being split into complementary genders," he reported. "Two of them said they hadn't, but the third one was startled by the question. His face grew red, and he began to fidget. Then he challenged me warily, 'Why do you want to know? Have you discovered something?'

"I told him I'd heard a rumor from a neighbor, which couldn't be true since there are regulations against such things. He snapped back at me, 'Why did you ask me if you thought there was no truth to it?'

"I replied offhandedly, 'I don't know. It was such a strange rumor, I guess it made me curious.'

"Then he betrayed his innocence by saying, 'Promise me when you find out what's happening, you'll leave my name out of it. I don't want anyone to think I leaked anything to you.'"

"He as much as admitted something unethical is being done with children!" I exclaimed. "Just as incredible, his sole priority was protecting himself."

"True on both counts," Luke agreed. "First I'll find the boy and make sure both children are safe. They can remain with us if they choose or be placed with another family. Either way, I want to guarantee they are together permanently. Then I'll determine how such splits are happening with children."

We looked in on Anna, who was sound asleep, the lavender bouquet by her bed. "Please, dear ones," I prayed, "tell us what we need to know to bring you two together."

I returned to my healing center the next day, taking Anna with me. Soon she was happily ensconced in a small cubbyhole used for storing herbs. New art supplies and developmental games kept her busy and contented.

As we ate lunch I asked, "Do you need anything else this afternoon?" If so, I can get it before the next patient arrives."

"I'm fine," she said. "But I was wondering, when we find my brother may I give him some of my materials? He might feel sad since I have so much and he has nothing."

"I'm glad you want to share," I acknowledged, "but we can buy special supplies for him. That way he can pick out what he wants."

"That's even better," she cheered, "then we can be sure he likes everything."

My staff took Anna under their wing, asking me no questions about how she came into my life or how long she would remain. They alternated teaching her lessons and keeping her occupied with creative projects. All four of us tutored her, and she thrived on the contributions each of us made to her learning.

I continued to grow the herbs and plants my healing practice required. As the number of patients increased, I needed more supplies than I could produce on my own. I rented an empty plot of land near our house and trained a retired couple in the care and feeding of every plant. I also taught them to listen for how each one wanted to be put to use. They did so and discovered valuable new purposes for the herbs.

The cycle of life was being honored through this natural approach to health. Each plant had the potential of being grown in perfect harmony with its divinity. We honored its purpose during the cultivation process and later as we mixed and administered a growing variety of herbal combinations.

Bringing every aspect of the healing process into alignment achieved optimal results. Harmony between the plant's divine intention and an individual's need enabled us to create an infusion tuned to each physical body. This often led to spontaneous healings, for which I thanked the plants profusely.

I followed one great truth: When all is aligned there is unlimited opportunity to create anew in divine perfection.

Such was the joy of my work and my life.

∞ ∞ ∞

Anna blossomed like a rose in the spring sunshine. She was a different person each day, constantly integrating new discoveries. Already she was a voracious reader and an attentive listener.

She ran to Luke every evening when he arrived home, hugging his long legs and bursting with stories about her day. He would pick her up, carry her to the kitchen, kiss me hello then sit down with her while she told him about one adventure after another.

Since we were conscious not to spoil her, we made it clear that on occasion Luke and I could be together without her. Once we explained this to Anna, she accepted it as fair and reasonable. I don't recall a time when she complained about a private moment we were having, except for a few adolescent tantrums a decade later.

Thus our family, temporary or otherwise, adopted an easy way of relating. I refused to worry about what might happen next.

Luke was trying to find the boy and, equally importantly, to determine if in fact children were being used in experiments. One evening after we put Anna to bed he revealed, "I believe the boy is being kept on the compound where I work. The boys are housed separately from the girls. The official story is that these children are either orphans or offspring of adults participating in experiments. However, I've only seen staff members who are pregnant. Women participating in experiments don't get pregnant, either because they have no access to men or because it's been permanently prevented.

"Soon I can start interviewing a few boys and girls to generate baseline data for a new line of research. My methodology has been approved. In less than a month I should be able to tell you if the boy is there, and what is being done to him and the other children."

"That's great news," I replied. "When you're with the girls, see if you can locate a caretaker named Anna. I never thought to tell you this, but when I first found our Anna, I asked what her name was. She said she had none. I told her she could have any name she wanted, and she chose Anna for the woman who comforted her when she was separated from her twin."

"So if I happen to meet someone named Anna, I'll find a way to tell her about another Anna," Luke declared. "She may also help me find the boy."

"Be careful," I urged. "You have two of us waiting for you at home now."

"And soon there will be three," he said with determination.

"I certainly hope so," I replied.

A few weeks later Luke burst into the house after work and told Anna he needed to talk with me briefly. He handed her a story to read and sent her to the patio with promises to be with her shortly.

"I met Anna!" he exclaimed. "She was bringing two girls into the research area, and I overheard one of them say her name."

"What did you do?" I asked excitedly.

"I introduced myself and asked if there was another Anna on the staff," Luke said. "She was the only one. I inquired if she would be picking up the children later, and she said she would be. When she returned I pulled her aside and told her, 'The girl who ran away is happy, healthy and safe with a loving family. Thank you for what you did for her while she was here. You were her only source of comfort and nurturing.'

"She looked at me with such surprise, I was concerned she might betray my confidence. But she quickly regained her composure.

"'You've given me a gift today,' she replied. 'I've been so worried about her. When she wasn't found, I presumed the worst. Thank you for informing me she is alive and well. But tell me, how did you know about my connection with her?'

"I recounted that when the girl was given the opportunity to choose her own name, she said she wanted to be called Anna after the person who cared for her. Then I asked if the institute was still looking for the girl."

"'As far as I know they gave up the search,' she reported. 'It was a halfhearted attempt to begin with. She was considered troublesome, and no one really wanted her back. They also determined she would be no threat to the institute since she doesn't understand the split she experienced.'

"Then the most incredible thing happened. When I inquired if she knew the whereabouts of Anna's twin, she told me I interviewed him that morning."

"You found him! Now what?" I asked expectantly.

"I'll suggest a boy and a girl be selected for in-depth observation. You know who the boy will be," he revealed.

We heard a small but insistent voice from outside. "I'm done with my book," Anna announced. "Can you come out now?"

∞ ∞ ∞

Luke and I spent hours discussing how he could manage to get the boy away from the institute, even briefly. We decided the best alternative was to request approval for him to visit us then gradually build a case for him to live with us permanently.

We were walking on the beach, Anna a bit ahead gathering seashells, when Luke and I each received an identical insight about how to proceed.

I spoke first. "I got it! You can report to those in charge that although the boy appears to be mild-mannered, he is actually a repressed troublemaker – a rebel in the making. That enables you to express serious concerns about his value to the institute going forward. You might also predict he could become violent and out of control."

"I had a similar thought," Luke replied. "I'll give them time to review my findings. Someone will identify his twin, also perceived to be problematic, which will validate my assessment of the boy. When the time is right I'll offer to become his guardian, explaining that we're unable to have children. Hopefully that will arouse no suspicion."

I did nothing to get ready for the potential arrival of the boy, mainly because I didn't want Anna to know we were making preparations for him. If our plan turned out to be unsuccessful, she'd be devastated, as would I.

A few weeks later Luke burst through the door after work with more exuberance than usual. He tended to burst in frequently, given his excitement about being home with "his girls." This evening we heard another set of footsteps accompanying him. Anna put down her book, I abandoned the herbs I was chopping, and we rushed to greet him.

When Anna saw the young boy with Luke, she screamed and ran toward him, her arms wide for an embrace. He looked perplexed, apparently not recognizing her. Her exclamations of, "It's my brother! My brother is home!" brought delight to his face.

Anna was jumping up and down, hugging and kissing him all at once. He seemed frail and timid, more prone to solitude than rambunctious activity. Embarrassed by her display of affection, he looked as if he wanted to run to the nearest closet and hide.

"Anna and Grace," Luke announced casually, "this is Jesse. He'll be staying with us a few days so he can enjoy fresh air and sunshine at the beach. Anna, I haven't been able to make arrangements for him to remain with us longer than that. If Jesse enjoys himself, perhaps he'll ask to come back for another visit. Then I'll do my best to make that possible."

Luke had successfully pre-empted Anna's likely assumption that Jesse had arrived in the household for good. She understood he would leave after a brief stay and return only if he wanted to. His choice, not hers, would chart his own future.

This was the first of many such instances when Luke found it necessary to clarify the boundary between Anna's perception of what was best for Jesse and what he wanted to do himself. Luke had established the primary ground rule for the enduring relationship between Anna and Jesse. We returned to it countless times over the years.

Gradually Jesse became more comfortable in his new surroundings. He said little, partially because Anna was so busy providing context for absolutely everything and partially because he was not naturally verbal. His life was controlled and constricted, whereas hers was expansive.

Jesse's way of relating to her was touchingly sweet. Clearly he loved her and looked out for her, albeit subtly. He was patient with Anna's constant interruptions and effusiveness, and his respect for her was evident in everything he said and did.

I watched how they played together as if they had actually been born five years ago and grown up together. They knew each other's character and personality intimately.

"Just like us," Luke said quietly, coming up behind me as I observed them in the garden. "They are mini versions of you and me, except for one significant difference. We're here because our original spirit made the choice to undergo a shift, and they're here because someone else made that decision for them."

"It's unfortunate," I concurred. "But if they can become a part of our family, their inauspicious beginnings won't matter. I'd love to wake up one morning and know they are with us for good and can never be taken away."

"I'm trying to move things along without calling attention to myself or Jesse," Luke replied. "Getting permission to bring him here was the first step.

Although it was a long time coming, this visit represents an important breakthrough."

"What's next?" I asked.

"I've alerted the officials at the institute that Jesse has a tendency to withdraw, which is often a precursor to rebellion," Luke explained. "I will report that it's likely he will become even more problematic over time. Hopefully at some point the program manager will be glad to have us take him off their hands."

"Does anyone suspect an ulterior motive?" I wondered.

"I've already stated my ulterior motive," Luke said. "I intimated that you are distraught over your inability to have children. I will assert it would improve my home life if we took the boy."

"As for Anna, I plan to petition for her through different channels," Luke continued. "I will obscure any connection between her and Jesse. People can believe they grew to love each other as brother and sister in the course of living with us. It's safer that way."

∞ ∞ ∞

We were sitting together on the first evening of Jesse's next visit. Luke and I were reading, and the children were sorting seashells. Jesse looked up and asked Luke, "Could I come to live with you and Grace and Anna?"

"We'd like that very much," Luke replied. "But wanting it to be so and making it happen are two different things."

"Why is that?" Jesse pursued. "I've dreamed ever since my first visit that I was living here. I'm always surprised in the morning when I wake up and see I'm still in the dormitory with the other boys. Why can't I be with you, if that's what we all want?"

"It may be what we want, but it's not necessarily what others want," Luke explained. "You're living at the institute because the people in charge believe you should be there. They would have to give their approval for you to live somewhere else."

"I don't understand," Jesse replied, bewildered. "It's my life, and I should be able to live where I want."

Anna listened intently, saying nothing.

"One day when you are older, you'll be allowed to make your own choices," Luke promised. "But for now, even if you don't agree, adults can decide for you."

Jesse was crestfallen. His champion hadn't accommodated his wishes.

"Let me see what I can do. Perhaps I can convince the right people to let you live with us," Luke suggested. "I have some ideas about how you can help the process along."

"Tell me," Jesse begged. "I'll do anything."

"Talk with others as little as possible when you go back," Luke advised. "We want everyone to know how unhappy you are. Don't say a word about wanting to live with us. Just make sure everyone knows you are sad and prefer to be left alone."

"Being sad won't be hard, since I am anyway," Jesse pointed out. "What else can I do?"

"Believe in your dreams and don't lose hope," Luke responded. "Even if it takes longer than you want, you'll be with us."

"That's also easy, because my dreams *are* real," Jesse stated.

"They are real because they are giving you a glimpse into how your life will be," Luke verified. "Now to bed.

Tonight you won't need to dream about being here because you *are* here!"

The next morning Anna approached me, clearly troubled. "It's not fair!" she exclaimed. "I made my own choice, and when I decided to go away I was allowed to. Now Jesse wants to leave and he can't. That's wrong."

"First off, you weren't allowed to leave," I countered. "You escaped. If anyone had discovered you on your way out, you would have been severely punished. They looked for you for a long time after you ran away."

"But I did leave, even if I wasn't supposed to," she persisted. "Why can't Jesse just escape too? He knows where we live. He could come straight here."

"Everyone knows he likes being here," I explained. "This house is the first place they would look. Then they might recognize you while they're at it, and you both would have to go back. It's too risky for him to slip out right now."

"Poor Jesse has to go back to that bad place!" Anna protested. "I don't want him to."

"Neither do we," I assured her. "But our plan has a better chance of working if we are persistent and positive."

"What is persistent?" she asked.

"It means we must commit to doing everything we can, again and again," I replied, "and more importantly, not to lose hope if we encounter an obstacle or two."

"I'll never lose hope," Anna declared emphatically. "I can be persistent."

"You are one of the most persistent people I know," I observed. "And because of that, you can help us accomplish what is required for Jesse to live with us."

Initially I was concerned the visits would harm Jesse if we failed to bring him into our home permanently. But I gained confidence in his strength and resilience. Under his delicate, almost ethereal exterior lay the heart of a warrior, and a peaceful one at that.

Anna amplified his courage by being positive and persistent. The more optimistic he became, the more he enabled Anna in turn to believe they could both live with us.

Their relationship was a reflection of the same interpersonal dynamic that existed between Luke and me. When I was thriving, so was he. When something was troubling him, I felt it even if he made no mention of it. When one of us committed to a purpose, the other exhibited equal dedication and responsibility. When one of us stumbled, the other was there to provide balance and stability.

I was aware of Luke's deepest inner tides as if they were my own, even when his emotions remained unspoken. I empathized completely, and yet I was never tempted to adopt his feelings. The line between what was his and who he was, and what was mine and who I was, remained inviolable.

We drew Anna and Jesse to us with our love. Other couples conceive their own children from their love, and so did we. The two children we brought into our lives were younger versions of ourselves, just as babies are of their parents.

For the moment, though, there were only three of us, and even Anna's place in our family remained in question. We coped with that uncertainty by strengthening the love that bound us together.

∞ ∞ ∞

"I've applied for a transfer of Jesse to our home on a six-month trial basis," Luke announced. "It's been taken under advisement, but I've been told the request will most likely be approved.

"I suggested a trial period to underscore my uncertainty about whether Jesse's apparent instability would create problems for us. My colleagues believe I'm making a great sacrifice bringing him into the family to assuage your grief over being childless."

"They have no idea who I really am, do they?" I asked.

"They don't, thank goodness," Luke responded. "Nor do they have any idea who I am. I intend to keep it that way. While they see me as a harmless researcher always finding the good in others, I can uncover the secrets they protect."

"You can be the purported stargazer, and I'll be the incessant hand-wringer," I laughed. "That should keep them entrenched in their typecasting. Meanwhile, we have the great joy of making room for another member of the family."

I had been pondering how to create space for Jesse. We made temporary arrangements for his visits, but they were unsuitable for the longer term. Every time I came up with an idea about what we could rearrange, I had to admit it wouldn't work. The cottage was not spacious enough.

Later that evening Luke and I were discussing when to expect Jesse to be released into our care. "Sometime next week is my guess," Luke predicted. "Soon we'll need a larger home."

"I was thinking the same thing," I said. "It took you two whole days to find this house, and it's been ideal. I wonder what you can find in the next two days."

"I don't need two days. I've already discovered what might well become our next residence," Luke revealed. "This time, though, you'll be fully involved in the decision about whether it is right for us. I might have succeeded in discovering this place all by myself, but I don't want to press my luck."

"How did you find it?" I coaxed.

"About a month ago I participated in a research trip to the other side of the island," Luke explained. "On the way back we got lost. The roads weren't well marked, and I hadn't paid attention to the route we had taken. So I was of little help.

"We turned onto a small road in order to get our bearings. That's where I saw a sign indicating the property at the end of the lane was for sale. I asked the others if I could take a few minutes to check it out. No one cared. They wanted to stretch their legs anyway.

"As I rounded a curve I saw a beautiful building on a finger of land surrounded by a beach on three sides. It was a substantial property, with sizeable grounds and an exceptionally large residence. I walked up and knocked on the door.

"I was greeted by a monk who told me the building had recently served as a sanctuary for aging priests. But with the newest technologies that slow the aging process, there was little use for the place. I could see us living there the moment I laid eyes on it."

"What about the monk?" I asked. "Does he come with the house?"

"He has been living there alone, tending the gardens and maintaining the property," Luke replied. "We might consider inviting him to remain with us."

"Can I see it tomorrow?" I urged.

"I arranged for us to take a tour in the morning," Luke replied, smiling broadly.

"That includes Anna, I assume," I clarified.

"Three of us will go, in anticipation of the arrival of the fourth very soon," Luke assured me.

"One final question, perhaps the most relevant one of all. Can you find your way back there?" I teased.

"You don't think I would discover our home after getting lost, only to get lost trying to locate it again!" he laughed.

True to his word, Luke took us directly to the property, which was owned by the Temple of the Divine Masculine. Whatever purpose it served at one time was apparently no longer relevant.

When I viewed the residence from a distance, I knew we would live there. Still, I didn't appreciate what an imposing structure it was until I saw it up close. Four wings converged in the center, where there was a sizeable living and dining area. Huge doors opening onto the outside from every room contributed to the spaciousness of the place. High ceilings made the rooms even more expansive.

I had no idea what we would do with a sprawling sixteen-room home, but I figured all that space would be put to good use. Anna and Jesse could have their own rooms in one wing, Luke and I would settle into another wing, and the purpose of the other two remained to be seen.

Tomas the monk showed us around the gardens. Although he was elderly, he was physically fit and full of energy. I wondered if he was living there by choice or by circumstance. If it was the former, he might not welcome the intrusion of a family with two children. If it was the latter, we may be able to convince him to stay.

During one of our subsequent visits I approached him about it. "Please consider remaining here," I suggested. "A boy Anna's age will be with us as well. As you can see, we are a young family. It would be a joy to have you share this home with us."

"I wasn't sure what would become of me when the house sold," Tomas replied. "So I did what I always do. I prayed and quit worrying about it."

"You will stay, then?" I asked eagerly.

"If you are sure you want me to," he answered humbly.

"We are certain of it," I replied, grasping his hands to keep from hugging him. "Welcome to our family, Tomas."

He wept. I forgot all about decorum and hugged him anyway.

Weeks of detailed preparation were required before the move. We notified the couple who loaned us their home that regrettably we were leaving. Then there were the inevitable tussles with officials representing the temple hierarchy, who felt the need to prove their worth by overcomplicating the purchase. Last but certainly not least, we took official steps enabling us to welcome Jesse into our family.

The property was sold as is, which meant the furniture and other contents would remain. That was fortuitous, since we had very little of our own. I offered to take stock of each item to determine what we would keep.

I scrubbed and polished everything in sight. It was like being on a treasure hunt. Extraordinary pieces were tucked away in unassuming locations: an ornate marble altar carved with ancient symbols; an alabaster jar of such fine quality, it was translucent in the light; a reclining chaise bedecked with imaginary animals and topped with a rainbow of cushions; a box inlaid intricately with mother-of-pearl.

Unable to contain my curiosity, I approached Tomas. "The furnishings here are rare and of remarkable quality, and some are rather strange for a residence. Where did they come from?"

He watched me intently, apparently debating whether to be candid with me.

"Now that you are the owner, you deserve to hear the history of this place," he began. "It was designed and built over a century ago for use by high priests when they came together to worship the many forces of Nature. This particular location was identified as a powerful vortex, since it is almost completely surrounded by water.

"About fifteen years ago an uprising occurred here. A cabal of renegade priests threatened to overthrow the high priest and establish their own rituals. They were intent upon replacing divine light with dark forces, using secrets of the order for reprehensible purposes. They wanted to control humanity by misusing the powers they learned in the priesthood.

"When their plan was uncovered, they denied any wrongdoing. Then that night they attempted to assassinate the high priest and others in influential positions.

"Thankfully, I overheard the traitors and warned everyone in advance. The priests used their spiritual capacity to emanate an intense magnetic force field. When their murderers approached them with weapons at the ready, they were electrocuted. I saw this with my own eyes. The priests' protective light was blinding in its power and brilliance.

"Afterward additional conspirators were uncovered. They represented two temples that had already been identified as centers of possible corruption. Horrible rituals were being performed there, all in the name of divine worship. The perpetrators were immediately removed. Those with the potential for rehabilitation were given an opportunity to show their merit. Then the temples were destroyed.

"The most exceptional pieces from both temples were cleansed of negativity and moved to this location. The priests ceased convening here and turned the residence into a resting place for monks at the end of their lives."

"Have there been any more uprisings or abuses?" I asked.

"I've heard of none," Tomas replied. "But then, I've been removed from temple intrigues and scheming for some time. I prefer it that way."

I filed away his last comment. Intrigues and scheming are not what one would expect to encounter where powerful spiritual practices are performed. I'd definitely discuss what I learned with Luke.

That evening we shared a delicious buffet prepared by Tomas. He had a wizard's insight for combining flavors and herbal essences. When we asked for second helpings, he smiled with pleasure. A priest, a gardener, an historian and a cook rolled into one had come along with our new home.

After Luke and I selected the wing for Anna and Jesse, we let them choose which room they each wanted. No one was surprised when they decided on quarters next to each other.

Tomas elected to remain ensconced at the end of the most distant wing. It gave him better access to the sea and his gardens, both of which he loved dearly.

Luke and I moved into the suite originally designed for the high priest. It had a large sitting room opening directly onto the ocean. The gold inlays in the mosaics were surreal. When the sun's rays shone on them, the floor undulated like waves on a calm sea.

Next to the sitting room was the bedroom, complete with a large platform bed that had an intricately carved marble headboard and posts with otherworldly patterns and geometrics. Fresh linens and a comfortable sleeping pad made the bed a welcome spot for our evening respites. The room also featured a massive ebony chest, a table inlaid with silver and ivory, two large chairs for reading and, once again, doors opening onto the patio, a garden and the ocean.

I was thrilled. I was home.

∞ ∞ ∞

We decided to search for a live-in tutor to teach the children while Luke and I were at work. At first Anna and Jesse resisted the idea. They were unencumbered by a schedule or any responsibilities other than being together, romping in the garden and in the surf. Luke and I allowed them time for that, but we also wanted to create a structure for their learning.

A tutor appeared soon after we agreed it was time for their education to begin. Erika came to my healing center for herbs to help her frail elderly aunt, who didn't have long to live. During our consultation she revealed she would be without a home when her aunt was gone.

Both women were staying with relatives who offered to provide their housing while the aunt was alive.

"Do you have any special skills?" I asked, wondering if there might be a place for her at the center. We were always looking for compassionate caregivers.

"I am a scholar," she replied. "I've tutored children to support myself off and on. I grew up among educated priestesses, and I became so intrigued by the process of learning, I couldn't find anything else I wanted to do. I kept studying and hoping someday my knowledge would provide me with a means to support myself. But lately I've been so preoccupied with caring for my aunt, I haven't been able to search for work to sustain me after she is gone."

"What subjects do you specialize in?" I asked, turning our conversation into a job interview.

"Everything fascinates me," she replied.

"Do you know arts and literature as well as the sciences?" I pursued.

"All of those and more," she answered.

"I have an idea. How would you like to live in my home and teach a young boy and girl?" I asked impulsively. "We reside not far from here, in a private spot with a beach, gardens and plenty of room for you. You are welcome to visit us to determine if that is something you would like to pursue."

"I know you only by reputation," she revealed. "Everyone talks of your generosity and gifts as a healer. With all my soul, I'm certain I am to teach your children."

"As am I," I assured her. "You may begin whenever you are released from your current responsibilities. I'll give you directions to our home. If you can't get away until you are ready to move in with us, so be it."

Erika arrived on our doorstep soon thereafter with her bags and scholarly texts. Her aunt had transitioned almost immediately after Erika secured her new position with us. She chose a room in the unoccupied wing of the house, and the children's education began the next day.

Rather than complaining about halting their carefree lives, Anna and Jesse welcomed the prospect of learning whatever they wanted from Erika. Her knowledge was so broad, they could name almost any subject and she could teach them in depth about it. They also learned experientially, studying everything from tide pools and tadpoles to the architecture of the house. Life became an infinite series of discoveries for them, each one nurturing their own love of learning.

Erika fit easily into our extended family. She, too, had found her home.

Idyllic months passed. Each of us was pursuing something meaningful. When we came together in the evening to share the day's harvest of new ideas and fulfillment, I was struck anew by the perfection of the moment. I wanted nothing to change, unless it would bring us even greater joy.

Just before Jesse's six-month trial period was concluding, Luke whispered to me in bed, "Soon we'll have to file a formal request to become Jesse's guardians. I'm trying to forgo the usual investigations into the suitability of our family and our living circumstances. Hopefully the necessary approvals will require nothing more than getting signatures on official forms."

"Can anything go wrong?" I asked, concerned all over again.

"I hope not," Luke replied. "I've been unswervingly positive about my work, so no one at the institute should object to our petition. I can't tell you how many people have commented I look downright blissful."

"You are, aren't you?" I teased, kissing him playfully on the cheek.

"Never more so," he replied, kissing me back, but not so playfully. And that was the end of our conversation about Jesse.

The massive bed where we slept every night, and made love more frequently than ever, was in the center of the room, which was perfectly square. Thus the bed formed a square within a square.

The ceiling above the bed was vaulted in the shape of a pyramid. It was painted in gold, starting with darker hues at the bottom and gradually shifting to lighter tones until it became white gold at the apex. Embedded at the top was a crystal pyramid that shone above us like a star. It glowed day and night, energized by an unknown source.

The first night we made love in our new home, we experienced an extraordinary union. The next morning we agreed it must have resulted from our relief at finally having our own place, not to mention our own family.

This energy became stronger each time we came together. Our passion was so acute we would sometimes be in ecstasy before we even shared a kiss.

Over time our lovemaking took longer and became more indulgent. We experienced the ebb and flow of near orgasm, continuing in our heightened excitement for quite some time before we both surrendered to our shared release. Our spirits were swept into the apex of the pyramid, where we merged fully as one.

We become so adept at this, we remained unified in the apex for an extended period of time. When we returned to our bodies, we descended as slowly and softly as a feather, separating just before we entered our bodies.

Eventually it dawned on us that the room was designed expressly for lovemaking within the highest vibrational frequencies. We had heard of priests and priestesses trained to practice the art of uniting physically and spiritually within the energy field of the pyramid. Amazingly, just such a pyramid was in our own home – in our bedroom.

One night we began our lovemaking in a lighthearted way as usual. Soon we were overtaken by the insistent need to merge. It was as if a force outside ourselves was trying to get through to us.

We brought each other to a familiar peak of ecstasy, but there was also something unfamiliar about it. I opened my eyes and was startled to see that Luke had become the high priest. I was his high priestess, trained in the rituals of the lovemaking we were sharing.

We were experiencing the potency of absolute union with Source, just as the high priest and priestess had done before us, in that bed under the glowing pyramid. We were performing the most sacred rite, worshiping the divinity inherent in Creation by revering the divinity in each other. When we united as one, we also united in perfect oneness with our Creator.

I was lost for a long time – lost in my love for Luke, lost in our shared oneness, lost in our oneness with all that is. What I experienced as ecstasy earlier with Luke was only a spark compared to this conflagration. I imbibed the bliss washing over me, imbued with indescribable love.

∞ ∞ ∞

The children were thriving under Erika's tutelage, along with unlimited fresh air and sunshine. Rather than spending long hours learning and then being rewarded with a frolic on the beach, Erika approached teaching differently. Education and recreation merged naturally into a totality that occupied the children from dawn to dusk. They made no distinction between learning and play.

Tomas was essential to the functioning of the household, growing visibly younger as the months went by. When I mentioned it to him, he responded, "Children will do that to you."

Luke and I were working longer hours, made possible by Erika's supervision of the children and Tomas' culinary and caretaker skills. I wondered if we were both getting too caught up in our sense of purpose outside the family. But because everyone was doing so well, I dropped the thought without belaboring it.

One evening as Luke and I were relaxing outside, he commented, "Since our guardianship of Jesse was approved without opposition a while ago, perhaps now we can take similar action with regard to Anna."

"What will we tell them about how she came to us?" I asked.

"We'll tell them the truth," Luke replied. "We'll state that after you found her all alone we tried to locate where she came from. But she didn't know and had even less interest in returning there. We'll indicate this occurred a few months earlier than when she left the institute, so no one wonders if she is the lost child."

"And what if they want to talk to her?" I asked, concerned she might reveal too much about her origins.

"I'll review with her what is about to happen and how important it is for her not to remember anything that occurred before you found her," Luke explained. "In addition, I've learned hypnosis techniques that should work well on her. She'll temporarily forget everything about the institute and what happened there. Then after our guardianship of her is approved, I can reverse the process to restore her memory."

"What else have you learned at the institute, and are you using it on me?" I teased.

"Everything I'm using on you, you taught me!" he replied happily. "As far as the institute goes, I've learned that what people see is a reflection of what they believe. If they believe you are a do-gooder, they'll perceive your actions through that lens. If, on the other hand, they believe you are politically motivated and out to secure rapid advancement, they'll see everything you do as being calculated to achieve that end."

"And you appear to be the consummate altruist," I noted.

"How else could I have gained access to the institute's most secret database?" he replied.

"You *what*!" I exclaimed.

"I now have the security code to the files documenting all research done since its inception," Luke declared.

"Do they know you have this?" I asked.

"The most senior director gave it to me," Luke revealed. "He's been following my research comparing the power of spirit with that of mental suggestion. He thought having the historic data might help me reach a conclusion more quickly.

"I'm still familiarizing myself with the system and technology. It's complicated and poorly organized. Once I can navigate through it, I should be able to find what I'm looking for."

"Then what will you do?" I questioned.

"You and I will decide that together," he replied.

Luke's plans for Anna worked beautifully. On the basis of the officials' interview with her, they allowed us to bring her into our family. At last the fragments of our lives were coming together, forming a multi-faceted jewel of a family.

∞ ∞ ∞

Of the four adults, Tomas was the most complex. He combined prayer and faith with a methodical approach to life. Often when he seemed mystified by something, he would achieve an unexpected breakthrough and shift onto a new trajectory. His resilience was reflected in his mantra: "surrender, trust, accept."

Jesse was a younger version of Tomas. He tended to observe a situation before he engaged with it. But when inspiration arrived, he jumped fully into it.

Jesse and Tomas developed a bond soon after we moved into the new house. Jesse empathized with Tomas' earthiness and the spirit he brought to every task. Tomas nurtured the herbs and flowers, fruits and vegetables with infinite care for the needs of each one. He knew them as he knew people, resonating with their growing patterns and seasonal cycles. Tomas lived in accordance with the waxing and waning moon and the high and low tides. He embodied an organic approach to his garden as well as his life.

Tomas held himself to high standards, though he cut everyone else considerable slack. He arose before sunrise to meditate and welcome the sun over the horizon. He gave thanks for his food before every meal, naming the plants that made it possible. He offered rose blossoms to the ocean at sunset, intoning his gratitude for yet another day of abundance, good health, fellowship and joy.

Jesse appreciated this ordered approach to the day and mentioned he would like to join Tomas for his sunrise and sunset ceremonies. I suggested he ask Tomas if he could do so. He returned shortly, beaming.

"Tomas told me I could participate in the ceremonies any time I wanted!" Jesse exclaimed. "He also said it was okay if I slept too late in the morning or had lessons to complete in the evening. But I won't do this once or twice then get distracted with something else. I'll train myself to wake up in the morning and make sure I finish my learning exercises early. I don't want to miss a single sunrise or sunset."

"I'm confident you'll not miss even one," I assured him.

Before long Jesse was saying the blessing for the family at our meals and teaching us what he was learning from Tomas about sacred tradition, its alignment with Nature and the meaning of the various rituals the two of them followed together.

At first Anna resented Jesse's newfound interest and became jealous of his growing attachment to Tomas. But soon she realized that as Jesse became more outgoing, he was more open and available to her. She witnessed her twin's subtle unfolding. For that, in her sweet and generous heart, she gave thanks.

Anna attached herself more to Erika, not so much because she was a female or because Jesse had chosen Tomas, but because Anna had a quick mind. She learned rapidly and needed the constant mental stimulation Erika provided.

Anna was interested in all subjects. She pleaded for opportunities to learn, the way most children beg for sweets. Erika offered her unlimited access to new topics and discoveries. Since Erika herself was of a similar bent, the two of them explored new ideas together. There couldn't have been a better match.

From the beginning the children knew we weren't their actual parents, so they called us by our given names. That suited us, since we often acted more like grandparents than parents anyway – grandparents in their twenties, no less. We spoiled them both. If anyone is to be credited with their solid upbringing, it is Tomas and Erika.

In the evening the children loved to sit on Luke's lap, but not at the same time, and tell him about their day. He was unswervingly attentive, asking them details about their adventures and discoveries.

They came to me more for reassurance when they were fretting over a mistake or a mishap. Once Jesse accidentally cut one of Tomas' prized roses while he was pruning. He ran to me in tears, saying Tomas would never forgive him. When I asked what he wanted to do about it, he thought for a moment and replied, "I'll tell him straightaway and suggest we use the petals from that rose as our offering to the sea gods and goddesses at sunset tonight."

"Very well," I replied, "then do just that."

Jesse explained to Tomas what happened and suggested they give the rose to the sea that evening during their sunset ritual. Tomas agreed, then swept Jesse into his arms and gave him an exuberant embrace.

Anna depended on me for clarification about what it meant to be a girl. I didn't have the heart to reveal I had been a female only slightly longer than she. Mostly I wanted her to understand a girl could be anything she wanted, just as a boy could. Girls loved the same way boys did, learned the same way boys did and accomplished just as much as boys did. A greater distinction would show up later, when it was time to fall in love. And then, I told her, I would explain a bit more about those differences.

"But I won't ever fall in love," she stated.

"Why would you say that?" I asked.

"Because I could never love anyone but Jesse," she declared with finality.

I couldn't contradict her. Still, she thought of Jesse as her brother, and they were being raised as siblings.

I settled on an open-ended response. "You never know how you'll feel when you are older," I said. "You'll always love Jesse. But you may also love someone else in a different way. There is room for both kinds of love in your heart, you know."

Anna persisted, "But you don't have both kinds of love in your heart!"

"You are right about that," I replied. "And perhaps you are right about yourself as well. We'll just have to wait and see, won't we?"

With that she returned to the learning rooms to accost Erika with a different question, which may or may not have been as thought provoking.

∞ ∞ ∞

My healing center became so successful I opened additional ones in various locations. I developed training programs so the centers could be staffed with capable, sympathetic people. Although this turned out to be a greater undertaking than I anticipated, over time I was gratified by the results of my long hours and hard work.

We took a unique approach to health and healing. Technologies existed to tune the vibrational frequencies of the physical body so precisely disease could be prevented and aging significantly slowed. But these procedures were costly and had to be ongoing to be effective.

Beyond that, the individual played a passive role in the process. It was more like getting a machine repaired by a technician than honoring one's body with healthy daily practices. People would overindulge in destructive food, drink and activities then check into a facility to undo the damage. Rather than contributing to wellness, technological advances encouraged irresponsibility.

My healing centers adopted the opposite perspective. People coming to us for help were expected to take full responsibility for their health. The moment they walked in the door, they participated in their own healing, whether it involved meditation, working with crystals, doing stretching and strengthening exercises or relaxing with a cup of herbal tea. The compounds we created from the herbs we grew were available not as an isolated means of repair and rejuvenation, but as just one component of wellbeing.

I designed each center to be a warm, comforting place. Fresh fruit and spring water with special infusions were available to everyone. Sometimes a musician stopped by to play, or the baker up the street brought delicacies still warm from the oven. Each center was as much a neighborhood gathering spot as a place of healing. But then, a sense of community contributes immeasurably to healing.

The centers offered care at no cost to those who couldn't afford it. The mix of people we served was diverse, ranging from wealthy widows to children suffering from malnutrition.

Whenever someone asked me how I got started as a healer, rather than give them an answer they might expect, I revealed the truth. "I'm completely self-taught. I heard the plants in my garden tell me how they could be used in healing and then followed their suggestions. They turned out to be surprisingly effective. Before I knew it I had so many people coming to me for help, I opened a facility away from my house."

One day I told a member of my staff about Fortuna, who asked for my soup to alleviate her fever. She listened with interest then suggested, "Why don't we make healing soup?"

My response was immediate: "Great idea. Would you like to lead the way?"

Soon we were selling soup from kiosks and carts all over town. Within months we experienced such high demand, we had to search far and wide for ingredients that met our standards. That led to our decision to acquire land with rich soil so we could grow our own organic produce and additional herbs.

Generosity was our abiding value. The soup that remained at the end of the day was given away. People started lining up with empty bowls before closing time. Then a wonderful thing happened. Many who came to buy soup would pay double the price so someone waiting for us to close could have their portion right away.

We made more soup than we could sell so there would be plenty of leftovers. "We can't let anything go to waste," we said at the end of the day, filling empty bowls. "Thank you for taking this extra soup off our hands." People smiled in gratitude and moved to the side with their evening meal.

Over time as my businesses expanded, I began arriving home later and later. Although I made it a point to be there to tuck the children into bed, I would sometimes miss the evening meal. The irony of it eluded me. I was so preoccupied with making sure everyone else was healthy and well fed, I missed dinner with my own family.

Lying in bed one night, Luke observed, "You've been putting the interests of everyone else ahead of us."

"Do you really believe I care more for others than I do for you and the children, or Erika and Tomas?" I asked in shock.

He waited a moment, weighing the likely impact his response would have on me.

"Based on your behavior," he said in measured tones, "I have to say I do."

Those words struck a blow to my heart. Luke was right. I was pursuing priorities more important to me than my family. My actions proved it.

We lay in silence a long while. Neither of us slept, yet we didn't know what to say. An unfamiliar gulf existed between us.

Tears streamed down the sides of my face. I tried to hide the fact that I was crying, but soon I was overcome by sobs of regret. I was responsible for what happened between Luke and me, and everyone else for that matter. If I had it to do all over again, I would never have made that first pot of soup for Fortuna.

Luke reached over and pulled me to him. Tenderly he swept the hair from my face and kissed my wet cheeks, which made me sob all the more. His arms were secure around me. He held me patiently, wordlessly, as I poured out my sadness.

Finally the tears subsided. My breath came in quick fits, and my eyes were so puffy I could barely see. Still Luke held me. Still he was silent.

I curled into him as I did so often. I loved the warmth of his chest under my cheek, and the smell of him never failed to intoxicate me. Though I'll admit, between my stuffy nose and emotional turmoil, intoxication wasn't imminent.

"You know I love you more than ever," Luke whispered.

"But how could you?" I protested. "I don't deserve it."

"You deserve every bit of my love, and then some," Luke replied. "It's just that you are so giving and tenderhearted, you're trying to save the world. And in the process, you have little left for those of us who love you."

"I'm a terrible person," I declared, sobbing once again.

"I couldn't disagree more," Luke replied, wiping my tears. "You're a beautiful, generous, creative, spirited, gutsy woman, and I wouldn't want you any other way. But could you spend a little more time with your family being your beautiful, generous, creative, spirited, gutsy self?"

Those words and his steadfast love swept away my remorse.

"I've created a strong organization with many capable people," I observed. "It wouldn't be difficult to give them more responsibility and assume less of it myself. Perhaps I could even train someone to take my place. Then I could return to being the healer I was when I started, working just a few days a week. The rest of the time I could be here helping Tomas with the garden and Erika with the children. That would be such a joy."

We slept contentedly that night, confident the dawning of a new day would portend the rebirth of our family and our relationship.

PART THREE
RAMANI AND THEANDOS

Many people believe major change requires some degree of force, continually applied. Luke never used force, subtle or otherwise. He was gentle and comforting. He reflected back to me in few words and without criticism how my life had veered off course imperceptibly over time. He spoke simply and authentically.

Most importantly, he affirmed his love, neither in spite of my actions nor because of them. Love was the one unwavering facet of his character. Not far behind was integrity.

Anyone else would have blamed me for being self-absorbed, complained about feeling abandoned, expressed frustration over my lapse in good judgment, berated me for not continuing to put him and our family first. Instead, Luke encompassed me in his love.

My efforts to help others and give back to the community were not wrong or inappropriate. Rather, I derived so much meaning from my work I failed to see the fulfillment inherent in my daily life at home.

It didn't take me long to learn that what had absorbed my time and attention could easily be accomplished by others. Instead of floundering, staff members flourished without my involvement. Most likely my constant presence prevented them from doing their best.

The children were pleased to see me arriving home earlier than usual, and sometimes not leaving during the day at all. I joined them in their learning rooms, helping Erika with their lessons or reading stories aloud to them.

We took walks on the beach in the middle of the afternoon, Anna and Jesse gamboling in the surf.

After Tomas familiarized me with the garden, I began digging in the soil again. Whereas my knowledge of plants was mostly intuitive, he taught me a more orderly approach to gardening. Jesse often joined us, studying the birds, insects and other small critters living among the plants.

I refer to the garden in the singular, but actually the house was surrounded by a number of gardens. They were connected by a rambling path that started in the rose garden, wound into a terraced vegetable patch, meandered past herbs growing in huge pots and ended in a tropical feast of wildflowers with a waterfall, a pond and a peaceful sitting area. Tomas had designed and tended everything lovingly over the years. It was his pride and joy.

I began cooking again, inventing feasts for the family. At first the meals featured my signature soups, but they evolved into more elaborate fare as I experimented with unusual combinations of ingredients and flavors. Everyone gobbled up even my less successful efforts. (I recall a particularly odd rosemary and kumquat sauce.) Tomas welcomed my involvement in the kitchen, since it freed up time for him to putter outside.

Tranquility marked our days and nights. The children were growing up, Tomas was grayer but still vital, Erika engaged in broader scholarly interests, and Luke and I loved each other all the more.

Luke continued to pursue his investigations at the institute, although he revealed little about what he was discovering. Eventually he stopped talking about it altogether. Months went by without his saying a word.

One evening after dinner I asked him directly about what he was uncovering.

"You're aware that my updates have been less frequent," he noted.

"Yes, but I didn't want to press you for information," I responded. "Lately you've been visibly preoccupied. Has something happened?"

"I'm not sure I want you to know," he replied, uncharacteristically hesitant. "I have irrefutable proof that hideous atrocities are being done in the name of research. To stop them I must go public with the evidence I now have in my possession.

"I'll be discredited and denounced, of course, in addition to being thrust out of the institute. That doesn't concern me. I don't need a professional reputation to define who I am, and our livelihood is no longer dependent on what I earn. I have your success to thank for that."

"Being able to walk away from the institute does afford you the freedom to tell the truth," I acknowledged.

"Agreed," Luke affirmed. "But if I'm not given a just forum where I can present my case, no good can come from what I reveal. Worse, innocent people could be harmed by reprisals against them. No one has colluded with me in unearthing the facts I now have, but others might be wrongly implicated.

"Then there is the danger to me personally. If I were living alone, I would simply choose the most opportune time to make my case to the authorities. But I have you and our children to consider, as well as Tomas and Erika. If something were to happen to me as a result of my actions, it would be devastating for all of you. I also worry for your safety. One never knows how broadly the tentacles of retribution might extend."

"You're sounding as if there is no justice," I protested in alarm. "Do you really believe if you make an airtight case regarding abuses at the institute, you might be the one punished rather than the perpetrators?"

"You underestimate the impact of influence in the hands of the few, especially the degree of corruption in the upper echelons," Luke observed. "Those in control will do whatever is necessary to retain their position. If I reveal what I know and justice prevails, the evil doers would lose all they have gained through their abuse of power."

"And if justice does not prevail?" I asked, though I didn't want to hear his answer.

"And if it does not," he said, pausing several beats before resuming, "then I would be imprisoned as a traitor at best and executed at worst. Given prison conditions, internment for life may be a worse fate than immediate death."

"You risk so much!" I exclaimed. "You must have discovered heinous crimes if you might face such extreme punishment by disclosing them."

"The wrongdoing is broad-based, not isolated in one area," he revealed. "Unethical activities have been covered up for decades by hundreds of people. Thousands have participated in experiments as human subjects. I estimate that at least half of them have been severely damaged."

"Why has none of this been exposed?" I asked, appalled. "Might others have been silenced before their voices could be heard?"

"That's possible," Luke commented. "However, if others previously uncovered what I learned and let it be known, the head of the institute wouldn't have been so ready to give me access to the entire database."

"Obviously they trust you," I noted. "Beyond that, those in charge may be so arrogant from having gotten away with their deceit, they feel invincible."

"Something even more insidious may be lurking," Luke observed. "It's entirely possible they are so comfortable with their abuse of power, they honestly think what they are doing is in the best interests of humanity."

"How could they believe destroying the minds, spirits and lives of others serves the greater good?" I asked. "Can they really believe what they are doing is akin to providing free soup to the poor?"

"Their self-deception may in fact run that deep," Luke conjectured. "When delusion permeates the highest echelons of power and seduces those who come into contact with it, a type of mass hypnosis can result. People stop thinking for themselves and recognizing what is occurring in plain sight. They sleepwalk through their days, convinced they are in the right because they support the existing hierarchy. Those with influence insist they are correct, and anyone who challenges or disagrees with them is a traitor."

"This is the dark side of complementarity," I remarked. "Fallen consciousness can turn it into opposition, justifying the separation of people from each other and their divinity. The world becomes polarized with competing notions of good and evil, right and wrong, black and white, all of which destroy common ground."

"I agree. This is as much about the deterioration of the human condition as it is about misdeeds at the institute," Luke stated. "It's the saga of humanity, which revolves around one fundamental question: Given complementarity in the context of free will choice, will we evolve toward our divinity or devolve into self-serving corruption?"

"Luke, you cannot suppress what you know to be true out of fear for yourself or our family, or from a sense of powerlessness to prevail against duplicity," I declared. "If you believe you cannot change anything, the forces of darkness will overcome the light."

"I have my answer, then," Luke replied solemnly.

"Given what you know, you must speak out," I concluded. "You can select the most opportune moment and audience, but you cannot refuse to act. The die was cast the day you set foot at the institute. You must not allow those who have lost touch with their own spirit to diminish yours."

"You do me honor with your faith in me, and you honor me even more with your courage," Luke declared. "I'll proceed as you advise. But you must know if you were to suggest otherwise, I would reconsider. It's not an easy choice, to give myself over to right action at the potential cost of being parted from my family."

"Please don't think about that," I urged. "We'll take this one day at a time. I ask only to be forewarned when you are about to go public with your revelations. I will prepare for the worst then, but not before. In the meantime, I will pray for you and love you and feed you soup to keep you strong."

"And charm me often in bed?" Luke added, pulling me from my chair and planting a kiss on my cheek.

"I feel a sudden attack of charm coming on!" I exclaimed as he picked me up and carried me to our bedroom. We made love slowly and indulgently that night while others in the house remained contentedly asleep.

∞ ∞ ∞

Months passed, and Luke said nothing about his preparations or plans. Just when his silence was beginning to cause me more consternation than comfort, he approached me with a look that told me he was ready.

"It's time," he said quietly. "I'm going to testify before the High Tribunal tomorrow. No one knows the subject of my complaint. Since the evidence I'll be presenting is irrefutable, my charges can be dismissed only with lies.

"I've tried in vain to determine the degree to which those who serve on the Tribunal have been corrupted. Based on official records, they appear to be standard bearers of justice and upright protectors of those less fortunate. If instead they are participants in the power abuse that permeates our land, they are adept at covering their tracks."

A wave of dread overtook me. I had a terrible premonition that the worst was about to occur. I couldn't let Luke be ensnared by treachery.

"I have a horrible feeling about this," I said with a shudder. "Are you absolutely sure it is your only alternative?"

"I am," Luke replied. "I must take the information public at the highest level."

"Please let me go with you!" I pleaded.

"It will be a private hearing in chambers," he explained. "Three members of the Tribunal have been assigned to hear my argument. Once they learn of my charges, they will probably give the institute an opportunity to prepare a response. The more time the institute is allowed, the more likely the Tribunal is colluding with them."

"I'll wait outside during the proceedings," I suggested, "praying for your safety and a just outcome."

"That would be a comfort to me," he affirmed. "I've placed a technologically condensed copy of my report and complete documentation of my findings in a hidden compartment inside the chest in the corner. I want you to have this in case I am taken away. If the evidence I am presenting is confiscated and destroyed, I must know another copy exists. You need do nothing with it."

"Didn't you just say that tomorrow is an initial opportunity for you to present your case, after which the institute will prepare theirs?" I objected. "How might you be in danger? The investigative process would have just begun."

"If dishonesty at the top is absolute, my actions will be deemed treasonous and I'll be hauled off in chains," Luke said with an eerie calm. "This is the High Tribunal. They have the power to act decisively and conclusively, for good or for evil. We'll know how extensively deceit has spread by the end of the day tomorrow."

I didn't sleep that night, nor did Luke. I tried to no avail to keep from tossing and turning. Just as I was about to ease out of bed and tiptoe into the sitting room, Luke placed his hand on my arm.

"Please don't go," he whispered. "I need you with me tonight."

He drew me to him and covered me in kisses. With my own kisses I tasted the salt of his tears.

"Oh, my love, do you have to do this?" I cried.

"You know I do," he replied hoarsely, aware of the incalculable loss his actions might bring. "Love me tonight. Love me until first light, when we will leave together, perhaps for the last time."

We made love all night, tenderly at times and passionately at others, wrapped around each other between our long moments of oneness.

As the dawn broke, so did my heart. I had to give him over to his purpose.

Luke was quiet and composed on our way to the Tribunal, steadfast in his convictions. Surprisingly, I was equally so. My vacillation and fear over losing him were replaced by the firm knowledge that he was defending those without the capacity or power to do so themselves.

He was also serving the larger emanation of love that connects us all. Living in that love required Luke to slay its opposite.

We arrived at the center of the city, where the official buildings were clustered. Walking up the steps of the Hall of Justice, a wave of nausea came over me. "He'll be the one on trial," I thought. "They'll find him guilty to protect those he is exposing."

"Luke, you're walking into a trap!" I exclaimed.

"If that is so, you'll have conclusive proof of how deeply corruption is embedded," he replied evenly. "If I am taken away, and I may well be, remember that I walked into the proceedings fully aware I may be sacrificing myself. I have no other choice."

We ascended the steps silently and found our way to the chamber of the High Tribunal. If I allowed any words to tumble out of my mouth, they would only weaken his resolve. I remained silent.

We paused outside the chamber door. He embraced me fiercely. Tears welled up inside me, but I willed them not to spill forth until he was gone.

"I love you," I whispered. "May you be guided and protected."

"I love you with all that I am," he vowed, diving deep into my eyes. Then he released me and walked through the entrance.

I waited outside, pacing. I studied the murals on the walls, attempted to read a volume I had tucked into my bag, cried intermittently and became more alarmed as time passed. Suddenly I felt a stabbing pain in my heart. "No!" I shrieked within. "You can't do that to him!"

The worst had happened.

I turned toward the door of the chamber just as Luke was being led out, chains shackling his wrists and ankles. Seeing him in such a crude state of bondage pierced my soul.

"Now you know how deep the roots of corruption extend," he communicated to me wordlessly. "Do what you can. Do what you must. I love you."

It took all my self-control not to run to him, begging for his discharge. Instead I nodded and mouthed the words "I love you." Then he was taken away.

A gaping part of me left with him. I was barely conscious of the shell of my body, standing in the middle of a public forum. I have no idea how long I remained there.

A tap on my shoulder brought me back to awareness. An unfamiliar female voice asked, "Are you all right?" At first I was disoriented. Then earlier events flooded back in, and I began sobbing, grief-stricken. The woman led me to a bench against a far wall and sat with me until I regained my composure.

"Something terrible has happened," she stated simply. "May I be of assistance?"

I asked my heart if I could trust her. Broken though it was, it answered in the affirmative.

"You may accompany me home," I replied.

"Thank you," she responded with obvious relief.

On the way to the house, she asked nothing and I offered no information. When we were rounding the bend that led to the promontory and our home, she broke the silence.

"I know this place," she said. "I was here many times with other priestesses, when the priests had their gatherings."

She was a priestess? Her humble demeanor and ordinary garments indicated otherwise. We entered the house and stood together in the central living area.

"Thank you for rescuing me amidst my despair," I told her. "I would invite you to dinner, but I'm exhausted and must rest."

"It's been a trying day for you, to say the least," she said sympathetically.

"Do you remember a monk named Tomas?" I asked.

"Indeed I do," she replied. "He was a master gardener."

"He still is," I responded. "I'll see if he can show you around."

"I'd love that," she replied, bowing slightly. It was then that I noticed how beautiful she was. Everything about her was striking: her porcelain skin, her silky auburn hair, her delicate bone structure, her curves in all the right places, her sparkling eyes and ethereal radiance. Yet she carried herself with such understated modesty, I noticed none of that earlier.

I took her to meet Tomas, then excused myself and went to the sitting room to rest on the chaise. I would have taken a nap on the bed, but the linens were still infused with the scent of our lovemaking the night before. I couldn't have borne it. Soon I was fast asleep. Luke's spirit hovered over me.

"Take heart. I am alive," he whispered. "I've been locked in isolation in a high-security holding cell on an island not far from here. I don't know what will happen to me, but so far I've been allowed to live."

"Are you unharmed?" I asked in desperation.

"I am," Luke assured me. "Please listen carefully. Soon you will receive information regarding the documentation I left with you. Focus your energies on how you might get this evidence into the hands of influential people. Be extremely careful, and require everyone you meet to prove their merit. Don't lose hope. Our love makes anything possible."

Then he was gone.

I awoke and lay on the chaise contemplating his message, "require everyone you meet to prove their merit." Apparently whoever might assist me would be unfamiliar at first.

Three simultaneous impulses crowded into my consciousness: I must get Luke released. I must protect the children. I must place the documentation in the hands of someone who can stop the corruption.

Dismay was not far behind. What should I do first? Could I accomplish one imperative without sacrificing the other two? Was there any chance I could achieve all three?

I was so paralyzed by uncertainty I couldn't formulate a coherent thought. I'd accomplish nothing if I remained in this state.

Then my heart filled to overflowing, and I knew Luke had sent his love to reassure me and provide a measure of courage.

The authorities could imprison him, but they couldn't keep his love from finding its way to me. They could put him in isolation, but we would still come together. They could exert physical power over him, but they couldn't break his spirit.

They couldn't break my spirit, either.

I collected myself and walked into the central living area, where Tomas and the woman were talking quietly. I approached them. "Tell me a bit more about how you two know each other," I requested, hoping to glean useful information about her.

"We have a long history going back to before this beautiful structure was built," she commented.

That was more than one hundred years ago, yet she looked barely over forty. No doubt my astonishment registered on my face.

"You are thinking I couldn't possibly be that old," she observed. "My dear, I am quite a bit older than this house, even."

"But you look so young," I commented.

"I engage in rituals and practices that almost completely halt the aging process," she replied. "I also employ crystal technology for the same purpose, but only when there is no other alternative. I've become adept at recalibrating the impact of time on my vitality and overall health."

If her intention was to distract me momentarily from my haunting concerns for Luke, she succeeded.

"Did you come here often?" I asked.

"Yes I did, always admiring Tomas' gardens," she replied.

Tomas stirred. "You're not familiar with who your rescuer is?" he asked me directly. I shook my head.

"I am the high priestess at the Temple of the Divine Feminine," she revealed.

"I stayed there after the split," I told her. "It was an enlightening time for me, essential to my understanding of what it means to be a female."

"Such transitions are traumatic," she acknowledged. "You navigated through yours with grace, as is befitting your name."

"The priestesses were generous with their support," I noted. "They provided an invaluable beginning for me. There is something I must ask you, though. What were you doing at the Hall of Justice today, and why are you not dressed as the high priestess?"

"The high priest sent me to find you, and I adopted a disguise so as not to be recognized," she explained.

"How did he know what was occurring?" I pursued.

"He receives ongoing information from a variety of sources," she said elusively, "most of them in the spirit world. Beyond that, his personal advisers are well placed. They know more than anyone realizes."

"So Luke's actions haven't gone unnoticed?" I asked.

"Far from it," she replied. "Luke's purpose is to uncover the evil occurring at the institute and right the many wrongs perpetrated there. In doing so, he will serve as a catalyst for eliminating corruption in the highest echelons of government and society.

"In the temples we engage in practices that strengthen the emanation of love for the benefit of humankind. But we cannot succeed by ourselves. Others such as you and Luke are here to embody divine light in the face of its opposite. You have been generating light and love with your healing centers and soup shops. Luke has been gathering evidence no one else at the institute had the courage to acknowledge. As we anticipated, he took that information to the highest arbiters of justice, only to be incarcerated for his actions."

"You already know all about us," I comprehended.

"I do," she said simply. "In addition to your work, you and Luke have been magnetizing the power of the divine masculine and the divine feminine through your union, under the pyramid in your bedroom. Your beautiful home remains vibrant with the exuberance of your extended family."

"Shall we discuss how we might collaborate?" I suggested with increasing confidence.

"That is precisely why I'm here," she replied, nodding to Tomas to excuse himself.

"I have information that could cause the toppling of the entire governmental hierarchy, not to mention the institute, if it is placed in the right hands," I confided. "Luke gave the Tribunal his report and documentation. By now the evidence has been confiscated and most likely destroyed. But I have a copy as well."

"Luke believed the Tribunal might be as corrupt as the institute's leaders," she acknowledged, "and thus he prepared for the worst. I don't want to know where the documentation is hidden. I ask only that we make one more copy for the high priest."

A wave of insecurity overtook me. What if I did what she suggested, and the file was erased instead? All would be lost.

I closed my eyes, asking, "Can I trust this woman and what she is proposing?"

Then my inner knowing declared, "She is of pure intention. Take the required steps to place the evidence in the hands of the high priest and high priestess. They have the ability to use it wisely and potently. Act with strength of heart, and you will serve the purpose for which you were created."

When I opened my eyes, she suggested what to do next. "I know a trustworthy technologist who can assist us. I'll meet you tomorrow morning at your healing center next to the farmers market, an hour after sunrise. Bring the evidence in its current form. I'll take you to someone who can duplicate it. Then together we'll meet with the high priest. Please continue as if nothing has happened."

"Very well," I agreed. "I'll follow my daily routine. Would you like to stay for dinner and meet the rest of the family?"

"Some other time, perhaps," she declined graciously. "I have many preparations to attend to. I'd best be on my way."

"Would you like to be accompanied to the temple?" I offered.

"No, thank you. I know the way," she replied.

After she left I went to the garden to talk with Tomas. I needed his assurance that whatever he might have learned would not be revealed to anyone.

"I've already forgotten what I heard," he told me without my asking. "You and Luke are virtuous. As for the details of what you've been doing to right the many wrongs in this world, I know nothing. Erika and I will provide a stable home for the children until Luke is returned to us and you can once again focus on your family. Do what you must to obtain the release of your dearly beloved and, if possible, stop the wrongdoings that so compromise humanity."

"Thank you for being here for us," I said softly. "I'll tell everyone at dinner tonight that Luke will be gone indefinitely on a special mission. That's the truth. I'll give the children no indication that anything untoward has happened. We can both pray that Luke is released and safely returned soon."

"I was praying just that as I pruned the roses," Tomas replied. "With each snip I affirmed, 'May Luke arrive home before the next buds have blossomed fully and are cut just before their beauty ends.'"

"Bless you, dear Tomas," I said, giving him a hug of gratitude.

That evening I explained to Erika and the children that Luke wouldn't be with us for a while. Erika's look of skepticism was met with an almost imperceptible shaking of Tomas' head. Reading his signal, she launched into a discussion with Anna and Jesse about what they could do with the time they usually spent with Luke.

"She is such a dear," I thought, "always looking out for the best interests of the two most important members of the family. What would we do without her?"

The children would remain content even during these traumatic times.

∞ ∞ ∞

The next morning I was at the healing center before the appointed hour mixing an infusion to alleviate difficult breathing when the high priestess arrived. Once again she was wearing unremarkable gray attire.

"Have you had any second thoughts?" she asked.

"Not at all," I replied. "Last night while I slept, Luke and I came together as we did when we lived in the temples. I told him of our meeting, and he confirmed the correctness of the path you propose. He also informed me he is being left alone and has been neither abused nor interrogated. He believes those in power are trying to decide how to proceed. The most advantageous, self-serving alternative must not be obvious to them, or they would have acted by now."

"Let's pray they remain mired in their confusion," she commented.

We walked a few doors down the street and through an alleyway, stopping in front of an unassuming storefront with this sign: *New and Used Paraphernalia, Gimmicks and Technologies*. I experienced a moment of doubt then realized there could be no better cover for a gifted technologist.

The shop was crammed with myriad machines, bizarre inventions, strange tools and toys. Some were obviously antique, whereas others were decidedly futuristic. I felt I'd walked into a time warp. Considering the priestess accompanying me, perhaps I had.

A wizened old man parted dusty drapes hanging in the doorway to a back room. Bony fingers protruded from the frayed cuffs of a robe that had seen better days, probably decades earlier. Although his face was lined with wrinkles, his eyes sparkled with delight when he recognized the priestess.

"It's good to see you again," he said, welcoming her warmly. "How may I help you?"

"We have something extremely valuable that must be duplicated in such a way there is no question regarding its authenticity," she explained. "In addition, we want to take no chances that the data might be lost in the process. Can you do this?"

"May I take a look at what is to be copied?" he asked.

I handed the documentation to him.

"These files were made with leading-edge technology," he observed, "one that precludes tampering while copying. Whoever created them knew exactly what he was doing. I'm impressed, and it takes a lot to impress me. I'll get to work immediately."

"How long will it take?" I asked, uncomfortable about leaving him alone with the data.

"It all depends on a few details I can identify once I open the files," he replied. "My own technologies are more than adequate, but I may have to make minor recalibrations."

"Very well," I agreed. "I'll wait here until you can provide an assessment of what must be done."

The technologist excused himself and disappeared behind the drapes.

"I've been following your progress with great interest, long before you knew of me," the high priestess explained. "I am committed to enabling you to bring this situation to completion and, not incidentally, expand the influence of right action across the land."

"May we overcome the challenges that lie ahead," I vowed.

"We will succeed in the immediate case," she predicted. "But whether we save humanity from the seductions of darkness remains to be seen. Either way, we must accomplish our current mission first if we are to contribute in a larger way."

The technologist reappeared from the back room. "Good news," he reported. "I've identified the key to the code that was used. A duplicate is being made now and will require just a bit longer to be completed."

"Thank you so much," I sighed in relief. "How can I repay you?"

"A lifetime supply of soup, perhaps?" he suggested with a twinkle in his eye.

When he was done, I placed the original safely in my bag. The priestess tucked the copy into the folds of her gown.

I presented the shopkeeper with a certificate I created on the spot. It read: "For services rendered, a lifetime supply of Soup Shop soups." I signed and dated the document with a flourish.

"To your good health and happiness," I said, bowing to him.

"I accept both with pleasure," he replied. "As for the soup, I've been enjoying it ever since you opened a kiosk near here. It constitutes my evening meal. Thanks to you, I never go hungry when I absentmindedly work through the night repairing a vintage contraption or inventing a new one that will be considered vintage soon enough. Blessings to you both."

He returned to his work before we were out the door.

The priestess and I stepped into the sparkling early morning sun. "Allow me to make my way to the Temple of the Divine Feminine, and follow as if you have no awareness of my presence," she suggested. "We don't want anyone to recognize me and worse, infer we are together. If that were to occur, we could both be abducted and searched. This way at least one of us will arrive safely with the documentation.

"If anything happens to me, tell them Ramani sent you to see the high priest immediately. I arranged this in advance, in case our plans go awry."

"You are Ramani?" I asked hesitantly.

"I am, though only my most intimate familiars address me as that," she commented. "You, my dear

Grace, must always call me Ramani. And you may address the high priest as Theandos."

It took quite a while to make our way to the temple. Walking behind Ramani as we passed through the gate, I was welcomed by Luke's spirit.

"I remember a garden here," he said to me, "where I first laid eyes on you after desperately wanting to see you for far too long. We are separated once again, but we'll be together soon."

"Are you suffering?" I asked, unable to hide my concern.

"No more than one might expect in my present circumstances," he replied, revealing little. "I have all I need to survive until I'm released. Meanwhile, my spirit will accompany you on the mission that lies ahead. You're a convincing emissary and a persuasive diplomat."

"We're on our way to meet with the high priest," I explained.

"I know," Luke affirmed. "He and Ramani have been visiting me telepathically for quite some time. I kept them informed of the corruption I uncovered and how I documented it.

"I am optimistic they will take compelling action that catches people unawares. The stakes are high – higher than my being returned to you and our family. They are higher even than saving the people destroyed by dealings at the institute and thwarting the perpetrators. The stakes are nothing less than the transformation, or the complete fall, of humanity itself."

"So if I feel I am carrying the weight of the world on my shoulders, it's not unwarranted," I remarked wryly.

"I love that you can joke with me at a time like this," he replied.

"Who's joking?" I retorted, only half in jest. Then I thought, "When he is home again, I'm never letting him out of our bed."

"Who said I would want to be anywhere else, as long as you are there with me?" Luke quipped, apprehending my private thought.

Ramani approached me. "I must change my attire, and I ask you to do so as well," she advised. "We both need to be clothed in garments woven with the highest integrity, of the most precious materials and sewn with love in every stitch. That will help us serve the larger purpose before us."

We were escorted to a frescoed room where ethereal garments were displayed. Each one was unimaginably delicate and created with sublime artistry. After Ramani selected gowns and accoutrements for both of us, I was taken to private quarters where I was lovingly bathed, massaged and oiled. Then I donned the new clothing and jewelry.

Assessing the result in the looking glass, I could hardly believe the transformation. I was robed in a pale pink silk gown with a gossamer silver tunic. The two delicate fabrics moved together with such subtlety, they seemed to become one. A necklace of platinum, faceted crystals and rose quartz adorned my neck. My copy of the documented evidence was secreted into a hidden pocket. "If only Luke could see me now!" I thought.

"I can," he sighed, his spirit hovering over my right shoulder. "You've never been more beautiful."

I entered a reception hall where Ramani was waiting, wearing a gown woven of cream colored silk overlaid in gold. Her jewels were set in gold of the finest workmanship. She was resplendent, the very essence of a high priestess.

"Come," she encouraged. "Theandos awaits our arrival."

Silently we swept down various underground passageways connecting the Temple of the Divine Feminine with its counterpart. A familiar glow emanating from an undefined source provided soft illumination. It was the same luminosity that shone from the crystal pyramid embedded in the ceiling above our bed. Similar crystals were implanted in the walls of the walkways, energized most likely by pure love.

Priests in robes of various designs and priestesses in an equal array of garments, from the extremely simple to the incomparably ornate, passed us in both directions.

Two priests guarded the entrance to the Temple of the Divine Masculine. They looked more like wrestlers than men who meditated for hours every day.

"Welcome. Follow us, please," they stated formally.

One led the way, and the other walked a few steps behind us. We entered another series of tunnels, also lit by glowing crystals. The walls sparkled with sacred shapes created from mosaics made of precious metals. "This is more a museum than a tunnel," I thought as we made our way.

We emerged into the natural light of day, in a room overlooking the ocean. A marble-walled reception area featured velvet cushioned seating and intricate mosaics embedded in the floor. Through oversized doors I saw an even more substantial interior space. I imagined large gatherings occurring there, with hundreds of priests and priestesses in attendance.

Today, however, there were just two of us, accompanied by our duo of protectors. I looked around for signs of the high priest. No one was present except a rather tall man dressed in a simple robe caring for pots of blossoming orchids and begonias. I assumed he was a gardener.

The architectural similarities between this structure and our house were remarkable. Our residence was neither as large nor as ornate, but the same fundamental aesthetic and attention to quality typified both.

"I'm gratified you arrived safely," came a voice from behind me. I turned and saw the gardener approaching us. This couldn't be the high priest! Admittedly, he was handsome and well built. His voice exhibited an authority reserved for those accustomed to it. Still, where were the robes and trappings affirming his exalted office?

"Let's retire to the veranda," he offered, "where we can sip cool minted refreshments while we talk."

He took Ramani's arm with the familiarity of one who has done so for decades, and we walked through the doors leading outside. He stopped and turned to me.

"Grace, you're a welcome vision on this day," he said gently. "Ramani and I thought this more informal setting would be a good place for us to converse in private."

"I'm honored you would meet with me on such short notice," I replied.

"We've been preparing for this occasion for quite some time," he revealed. "Ramani and I have been aware of Luke's clandestine research. He came to us often during his meditations and hours of sleeping, keeping us fully informed. The three of us never met in person, however, nor did we overtly acknowledge receiving information from him.

"He collaborated with us in the realms of spirit in order to create the consummate contingency plan. When he gave you the technological files, he downloaded the same material to us telepathically. We carry it in our spirit consciousness, where it is categorically secure. He did so knowing if his efforts were thwarted and all evidence of wrongdoing was destroyed, we would still have the information he had uncovered."

"Why was it necessary to copy the files?" I asked.

"We must validate what we are about to assert," he explained. "I have many detractors who would claim anything downloaded from the realms of spirit doesn't represent reality. They would argue the evidence was falsified. We'll send the technological copy of the documentation to the highest authorities in government and assure them your original is safely concealed. Now, let's strategize."

During the ensuing conversation I felt I was talking with two close friends supporting me during a crisis. Not a hint of arrogance or conceit entered into our interaction.

"I'll review what we discussed," Theandos said in conclusion. "Grace, you'll return to your home and your various businesses, pursuing your daily routine. Make no mention of Luke's sudden departure. If anyone asks about him, explain that he's working on a special project. To assuage your concerns, I believe the people at the institute are so absorbed in impeding his actions they will not harm your family.

"Meanwhile, Ramani will gather her most adept priestesses and ask them to take turns meditating continuously to invoke the support of the divine feminine in this endeavor. I'll do the same with the priests here, who can invoke the divine masculine. We'll create the strongest vibrational vortex to protect those taking action to achieve the best result for the greatest number.

"We'll inform those in positions of authority that we have proof regarding the corruption and power abuse that overwhelm all aspects of government, justice, science and society. Then we'll announce that we are prepared to obliterate this darkness and all who perpetuate it, replacing it with divine light. We'll give them a brief period of time to decide how to respond. If they either attack or attempt to betray us with false promises, we will strike with the force of our light."

"We're engaged in a struggle to the death," Ramani asserted, "if not literally then certainly symbolically. Light must overcome anything that compromises or limits it. The time has come to use divine love as an invincible force, that we may stop the downward spiral of humankind into an abyss of divisiveness, cruelty and power abuse."

"I will insist on Luke's release and require that he be placed in charge of the institute," Theandos continued. "In addition, I will demand the replacement of anyone who chooses not to follow the light. I plan to employ resources in all the temples, including the power of prayer, meditation, contemplation, intention, harmony, chanting and spiritual union, to realign the magnetic frequency of mass consciousness. People might then insist on a return to integrity, and leaders will be well advised to embody it. That is our vision of the future. May it be so."

"May it be so," Ramani and I repeated after him.

"On a different note, I want you to know how many happy years Ramani and I spent together in what is now your home," he said, his countenance relaxing. "We built it as our residence, as well as a place where priests and priestesses could celebrate the union of the divine masculine and the divine feminine.

"The fact that you, Luke and your family now occupy that sacred dwelling delights me immensely. More importantly, you two are continuing the tradition Ramani and I honored there with our ritual lovemaking. Our purpose was, and continues to be, to spread the vibration of divine love across all of Creation, through the perfect union of the divine masculine and divine feminine."

"Could you explain the pyramid that glows in the apex above the bed?" I asked, choosing not to be shy about the topic at hand.

"It is infused with our love," he replied, looking at Ramani devotedly, "and will glow as long as love remains."

Then he took Ramani by the hand and helped her from her chair. Our meeting was over, and their further work was about to begin. "May you and your divine complement be one again soon, in this realm and in all others," Theandos declared in benediction.

"We offer you our love, our service and our gratitude," I replied. "May we grow to love as you do and serve as you do, in eternal commemoration of our Source."

"Peace be with you, my dear," Ramani replied. Arm in arm, they left the veranda.

I was allowed to remain alone, composing myself. After a brief interlude one of the priest escorts appeared in the doorway and announced quietly, "We've come to guide you back."

Returning to the dressing room, I changed into my own garments. I was about to leave when a priestess approached me. "Grace, don't forget to take your clothing and necklace," she said, handing me a satchel.

"I couldn't," I replied. "The gown is much too beautiful for me."

"Nonsense," she insisted. "It was made for you, precisely to Ramani's specifications. She designed the necklace for you as well, and had it crafted by her own personal artisan. They are her offering to you."

"Please inform her of my gratitude," I replied, "and tell her I accept her generous gift with all my heart."

She walked me to the temple gate, where the setting sun greeted me. I started for home with my precious cargo, which included spun silk, handcrafted platinum and technology with the power to transform.

That night Luke and I met in the nether realms as we slept. I told him of the day's occurrences and encouraged him to remain hopeful of his release. He indicated he'd already begun planning what he would do if he was freed and given the opportunity to manage the institute. Then our conversation took a different turn.

"So, my love," he began, "there you are in our bed alone and here I am, alone and lying on nothing even remotely like our bed. Nonetheless, we might be able to come together anyway."

He surrounded me in the cocoon of his love. It was so secure, so steady, so comfortable, I disregarded the fact that we were physically separated. I even forgot momentarily that he had been locked away.

I received his love fully within my spirit as I so often received him physically. At the moment of our perfect union, our energy rose to the glowing apex of the pyramid above our bed. Luke was not in prison and I was not asleep in our bed. We were unified in love.

Our love-based union was real, and our separation due to the forces of hatred and oppression was not. Our life was to be lived in the context of love, not its opposite.

We remained together in ecstasy throughout the night and parted reluctantly at dawn, preparing to awaken in our individual locations. Before Luke left me, he whispered something I will hold in my heart forever:

My love is eternal.

My existence is defined in partnership with yours.

My heart has room for only you.

My spirit embraces you with the wind.

∞ ∞ ∞

The next morning at breakfast Anna and Jesse expressed their concerns about Luke's sudden absence.

"He didn't even kiss us goodbye!" Anna protested. "He never leaves without giving us a hug."

"Besides, he promised he'd help me find new creatures in the surf," Jesse chimed in. "We were supposed to do that last night before the sun went down. But he wasn't here."

"He sends his apologies and wants you to know how much he loves you," I assured them. "He'll be home soon, though he doesn't know exactly when. Be patient, and perhaps Erika will give you something special to do each day until he returns to us." I looked at her pleadingly.

"Yes, absolutely," she said quickly. "I have a project for this afternoon. But if you'd like to start on it right now, that's fine with me."

"Yes!" the children cheered, jumping up from the table and following her into the learning rooms.

"I hope he's not gone too long," I said to Tomas. "It would wound the children terribly to think he abandoned them without a thought."

"Take heart, Grace," he replied. "I told you Luke would return before the last days of the perfect rose. It's barely beyond a bud. The work of courageous people, Luke and you included, will be accomplished successfully. Keep yourself busy, and leave the rest to Erika and me."

I did just that. Time passed more quickly that day. Before long I had tucked the children into bed and was preparing to retire for the night.

Something caught my eye from a chair across the room, where I placed the satchel from the temple. Incongruously, the bag appeared to be lit from within.

I walked over to investigate. There was no explaining this strange phenomenon. Nothing was above, behind or below the satchel that could create such a glow. It must be coming from inside.

I opened the bag and was almost blinded by light bursting forth from the necklace. Gingerly I reached inside. It was warm, like heat from embers in the middle of the night. The faceted crystals were glowing, just like the pyramid above our bed.

"Put it on," Luke's spirit urged. "Wear it to bed tonight so we may energize it with our love."

"How can I resist?" I replied. That night, and every night until Luke's return, we came together. Within the apex of the pyramid above our bed, we held our oneness until the dawn. The necklace glowed ever more brightly.

∞ ∞ ∞

Almost a month passed since Luke was imprisoned. Despite our nocturnal togetherness, I was becoming more frantic for his welfare during the day. How would I survive his lengthy incarceration? More importantly, how would he?

I knew the moment Theandos communicated his challenge and the war between the forces of light and dark began. I was talking with the manager of our soup shops about expanding the business when I felt something like a kick in the gut. "Are you all right?" she asked.

"I'm fine," I replied casually, "just the victim of too much work and too little sleep. Let's continue this conversation another time."

I excused myself and slipped outside for some fresh air. Ramani's spirit was hovering.

"Thus we begin," she said. "Please help us hold the power of the divine feminine."

I poked my head inside and asked my staff to allow me privacy on the deck. Then I met the priestesses in meditation in the nether realms. I also sought out Luke to help him support the efforts of the priests empowering the divine masculine.

At one point I heard myself repeating with my inner voice, "Thy will be done. Thy will, not mine, thy will be done."

In a moment of insight I understood the impact of releasing my willfulness. Detaching from the desire to control the outcome – affirming my faith in the benevolence of the Divine – asserted my ultimate power. Surrendering in such a way filled me with a peaceful inner knowing that whatever occurred would be divinely ordained. I prayed for the wisdom, courage and patience to continue trusting in Source.

Suddenly I felt an unimaginable force burst through an equally strong resistance. A wall of darkness had been penetrated, if not completely obliterated. Light was streaming into the murky corners of fallen consciousness. The final result was far from guaranteed, but the breakthrough we planned and prayed for had occurred. The priests and priestesses, working in tandem with their collaborators in the highest realms, succeeded in their quest.

I remained in a deep meditative state, alternating between visits in spirit with Luke and communing with the priestesses. An opalescent ball of light appeared before me, and the unified voice of Ramani and Theandos announced, "It's over. Light has overcome the darkness, and Luke is free. Bless you, our dearest one, for all you have done to make this possible."

I sent them a message of love and gratitude then drifted into nothingness. I was neither awake nor asleep, and surprisingly unconcerned about how and when I would find Luke after his release.

It was evening when I stirred and prepared to leave for home, hopeful Luke would make his way there soon. As I stepped into the street a shadow appeared against the door.

"Thank the gods you're still here!" It was Luke.

I held him tightly, sobbing into his chest. When I pulled away, I saw how weary and sickly he was.

"What have they done to you?" I cried.

"Nothing your powders and potions can't alleviate," he replied.

I used everything in my power and my collection of herbs to undo the toll Luke's terrible treatment had taken on him. All the while he described what happened during his imprisonment. It was so horrible it doesn't bear repeating.

He was somewhat revived when we started home. We tiptoed into the house so as not to awaken anyone, having decided to surprise them in the morning.

"Where is that stunning necklace?" Luke asked when we stepped into the bedroom. "I've seen it many times in my sleep. Now I want to see it for real, on you."

I experienced an unaccustomed onslaught of self-consciousness, concerned I might not meet his expectations. This was never an issue before. I always felt comfortable with Luke, whether we were reading together by the fire or making love in our bed.

"You are beautiful," he whispered reassuringly. "If you don't want to show me the necklace, let alone wear it, I'll feel blessed just to have you in my line of sight. If you would talk until morning to recapture what occurred here at home since you left me outside the so-called Tribunal of Justice, I'll revel in every word. It's such a joy to know I can reach out and touch you, nothing else matters."

Here was my beloved Luke, having endured untold tortures and threats, once again comforting me. It was I who should be comforting him, I thought, bursting into tears. I cried tears for us both: tears of relief that Luke was free and home once again; tears of rage over what he endured and the diabolical purposes behind his incarceration; tears of hope that perhaps the long reign of darkness was coming to an end.

I wore the necklace. Luke loved it.

I kept waking up that night fearing Luke had been taken from me. In the course of our lives together I came to depend on his steadfastness. Yes, I was a successful, independent businesswoman pursuing my own activities. But I always knew I could come back to him, just as I could return to his arms during our precious hours of privacy.

Now that he had returned safely, I was incapable of being strong. I was bereft at the thought, and the actuality, of losing him.

"Still worried?" he asked with his usual perceptiveness.

"I'm finally letting myself feel abject fear," I replied, "a delayed reaction."

"That happens after a monumental challenge," he commented. "When the intimidation dissipates, the person shouldering the burden often falls apart. Remember, though, just because you are experiencing fear now is not an indication I'm still in danger.

"No one can keep the truth hidden by suppressing me now, and they know it. To harass me any further would serve only to prove my point. I doubt anyone will come after me."

"What a relief," I sighed. "I can't wait to start healing those who were harmed by the institute while you focus research on positive ends. That's our work."

"I hate to disagree with you, my dear sweet Grace" Luke countered, "but that's not our work." Pulling me to him, he kissed me deeply and at length. "This is our work, and it's high time we got back to it."

"If you insist," I said, kissing him on his nose, his eyes, his expressive lips. "But I'll acquiesce only if you promise to be diligent at our task, most evenings, in order to assure our success."

"Agreed," he whispered, and we went about our "work" for the rest of the night.

The children were excited and relieved to see Luke the next morning, ready for a new day in more ways than they knew. Anna pounced on him first, settling into his lap.

"Luke!" she exclaimed. "Where have you been? I missed you the whole time you were gone and called out to you every night so you'd come home soon."

As always, Luke had the perfect reply. "I was accomplishing a very difficult but important task, and I'm happy to report it was successful. I too prayed every night that I would see your sunny, smiling face one morning just like this one, and that Jesse would be bounding up to me as well." He scooped the boy into his arms and gave them both a hearty hug.

"Now tell me, what have you been up to while I was gone?" Luke asked. They launched into their stories about star shapes in the sky, sand constructions and the process of metamorphosis.

Erika watched them in silence, studying Luke intently. Then she shifted from contemplation to conversation. "Tell us about the goal you set out to accomplish when you left," she suggested. "Anna and Jesse are learning about goals and how to achieve them."

"I went to an island off the coast, where I had to face my own fears in order to right a terrible wrong," Luke divulged. "It was unclear whether I would prevail, but I received considerable help, and we overcame the forces against us. Now I hope I can alleviate the damage done to many people and help them find happiness again."

Jesse and Anna listened attentively. Rarely had he been so grave. Resolve was palpable in his voice. He was the consummate role model, someone with a goal to serve others and the courage to make it real.

"I can't do this, of course, without the commitment and involvement of Grace and Tomas," he explained. "Grace and those who work at her healing centers will enable many people to regain their health. We all know her soup and healthful remedies work wonders. Combined with the herbs and other gifts of nature that Tomas grows in our gardens, I'm confident many unfortunate people will start feeling better soon."

"Can we help too?" Jesse pleaded.

"Yes indeed," Luke responded. "You and Anna can create illustrated stories for everyone to enjoy. Build aquariums for those who haven't seen the ocean in a long time. Make beautiful bouquets of flowers from our gardens to provide fragrance and freshness in the rooms where people congregate. Could you do that – and anything else you and Erika might dream up?"

"Yes, yes!" Jesse and Anna exclaimed. "Let's get started right away. Erika, can we spend the day working on these projects?"

"You can spend the whole week creating them if you want," she affirmed. The children hopped off Luke's lap and went running to the learning rooms, Erika trailing after them.

Tomas had been quiet, appreciating the scene he was witnessing. "I have one final task for you both to accomplish before you leave this morning. Follow me," he said. As we approached the rose garden, I knew what he was about to do.

"Luke, when Grace arrived home after you were taken away, she was distraught with the fear you wouldn't be released," he commenced. "I told her you'd be with us again before the bloom on this rose was in its final days of beauty."

He reached for a fully opened rose, swaying in the sea breeze. By evening its petals would be dropping to the black soil beneath. Tomas snipped the stem and handed the rose to me.

"Dry this blossom and keep it as a reminder that your love is eternal, so strong that even the most impossible separations are only temporary," Tomas advised.

"I bless the day you came into our lives, and I'm even more grateful you chose to remain with us," Luke affirmed. "Thank you for your wisdom and your love."

I took the rose to our rooms and placed it on the altar to dry in the sun and sea air.

∞ ∞ ∞

Just as Luke and I were about to leave that morning, a messenger appeared at the front door. "I am to escort you to the temple for an important meeting," he announced. "How long will it take to make yourselves ready?"

"Since your arrival is unexpected, we need time to prepare," Luke replied. "Please excuse us. We'll be back momentarily."

Luke and I adjourned to our rooms. We had already risked too much to leave with the first messenger at our door after his release. We lay on our bed, held hands, closed our eyes and concentrated our thoughts in the crystal pyramid embedded in the apex of the ceiling. Our objective was to discern the validity of the messenger's information. If indeed someone at a temple had summoned us, it was surely Theandos or Ramani. One or both of them would appear to confirm it.

In my vision Luke and I were discussing with them what occurred the day before and how to proceed. When I asked if they sent the messenger, they nodded affirmatively.

Luke opened his eyes and told me, "I saw us sitting with the high priest and priestess in an outdoor area. They verified that they called the meeting. And you?"

"I received the same validation," I affirmed.

"Well, then, let's not keep them waiting," he declared.

I wore my usual clothing, adorned by the necklace. A subtle glow emanated from the faceted crystals.

We entered the Temple of the Divine Masculine and were taken to a reception area where others were waiting to be admitted. Clusters of priests mingled with as many priestesses. Ordinary citizens were scattered about as well. Based on the sheer number of people who had assembled, I assumed our wait would be considerable.

Instead we were shown into a small private chamber where Theandos and Ramani were engrossed in conversation. Looking at them from the perspective of this new day, with Luke at my side, I saw how perfectly suited they were to each other. They were two halves of the same entity, both strikingly handsome. They shared a commanding presence and a casual intimacy. Fluidity between them evoked their oneness.

"Welcome," Ramani said, striding forward and taking my hands in hers. "I see you've energized the necklace. It's stunning on you. And this must be your beloved Luke."

I turned to him. "Luke, this is Ramani, who found me after you were taken away. Ramani, this is indeed my beloved Luke."

"What a pleasure to meet our most courageous emissary," she replied warmly. "My gratitude for the risks you took is exceeded only by my regret that you had to endure imprisonment."

"It was but a short time," Luke said modestly, "a small price to pay for the unmasking of corruption at the highest level of the judiciary and elsewhere."

He spoke openly, exhibiting a prior understanding between them of his purpose and the larger context for his actions. Clearly his spirit communicated with them before and during his incarceration.

"Thankfully you returned safely and are unharmed," Theandos declared. "We surrounded you with an almost impenetrable protective vibration from the time you entered the Tribunal chambers until you stepped into your home last night."

"You believed I might have been in serious danger then," Luke noted.

"We were certain of it," Theandos revealed. "We had visions of your being murdered before you left the Hall of Justice. We did everything in our power to prevent that, and something less severe, from happening."

I shuddered at the realization that Luke had been in such serious jeopardy. Ramani touched my arm lightly. "He's with us now and will be with you for decades to come," she stated reassuringly. "The worst is over. Let's plan what we are to do next."

Theandos led us to a table set with platters of fruits and cakes, along with a pitcher of pomegranate juice and four goblets. We took our seats and continued the conversation.

"We called for you to come here directly after Luke's return, because time is truly of the essence," Theandos explained. "We've only begun to eliminate the corruption that decays and destroys our society. Even so, we've succeeded in taking an initial, irrefutable stand that it cannot continue.

"We exerted our power in the form of divine light and love and managed to prevail this time. Nonetheless, the response to our actions will be violent. The forces of darkness will do everything they can to thwart our intentions and preserve power. We must act swiftly and decisively on a number of fronts to neutralize the influences that would destroy the light.

"The two of you are to be lightning rods for our work with the ultra-high frequencies of divine love. We will emanate extremely powerful vibrations from these two temples, and we ask that you ground those energies on the Earth plane.

"Anyone who decides to release their lower consciousness may enter the vibratory vortex we are establishing. It will enable them to access divine love and cleanse misaligned residue in their soul. This is an unprecedented opportunity for individuals to transform. After they have embraced the light themselves, people may use their free will to demand that corruption and abuse of power no longer be tolerated."

"That is where you come in," continued Ramani. "We cannot cause this transformation, for to do so would be to interfere with free will choice. But we can provide the most limitless, love-based context in which people can recapture their own divinity. We can also help neutralize apathy and cynicism throughout the collective.

"Your responsibility is to embody love, forgiveness and compassion as you pursue your daily activities. This will raise the potential for all to do so as well. You'll be given full access to emanations from the temples. As you integrate these vibrations into your being, you increase the potential for others to receive them. This capacity must reside within you first, however."

"And you believe we are up to the task?" Luke asked.

"We have no doubt that you are," Theandos affirmed. "Before you split into two, you were actively involved with us. You confirmed the consistent abuse of those participating in destructive experiments at the institute. You came to us with this information, and we began developing a plan with you."

"I remember none of this," Luke observed. "Does this sound familiar to you, Grace?"

"I have no recollection of it either," I revealed.

"Think of your arrival as two people as a rebirth," Ramani explained. "Just as a newly born child remembers nothing of the lives that preceded the current one, so was that memory temporarily lost to you. Each lifetime is an opportunity to begin anew rather than being slavishly bound to former patterns and past experiences. Even so, the residue of earlier perspectives, preferences and capabilities remains and can influence each person's choices."

"Luke, soon after the split you went to the institute looking for work and were hired right away," Theandos remarked. "Did you ever wonder why that happened so quickly?"

"The question did cross my mind," Luke acknowledged. "But such extraordinary things were occurring at the time, I assumed finding a position there was meant to be."

"Because you worked at the institute before, when you returned they recognized you on some level," Theandos noted. "We assisted with our prayers, and everything unfolded from there."

"Were you present during the process that accomplished our split?" I asked.

"We led the chanting that created the vibrational vortex enabling it to occur," Ramani answered. "I left just before you descended into the Merkabah as two in order to prepare the way for you, Grace. I created a pathway of divine light so you wouldn't be overly distraught at the prospect of immediately being separated from your beloved.

"You have more than met our expectations. The two of you are able to make a positive difference in the world individually. But when you come together, you are even more exceptional. We are gratified by the depth of your love."

"Was our house part of the plan?" Luke ventured.

"Not initially," Theandos revealed. "We intended to use that structure only as a place of ritual to enhance the vibration of love throughout humankind. But as you know, the sacred space we created was so violated it could never again serve its original function.

"Much later Ramani and I were meditating on the question of what to do with the property. We had been tracking your progress and were aware that you would be looking for a larger place to live. We arranged for your research expedition to get lost precisely where you could discover your new home. We also communicated with Tomas' spirit, encouraging him to make you feel welcome. The rest followed flawlessly from there."

"And the bed under the pyramid?" Luke couldn't help asking.

"We left it as we created it, fully magnetized for the alignment of the divine masculine and the divine feminine. That is our gift to you," responded Theandos.

"And what a gift it is!" Luke exclaimed.

"We're pleased that you are our inheritors," effused Ramani. "Beyond that, our collaboration is only beginning. The four of us have much to accomplish together."

"Let's get started, then," I suggested, to which she replied, "We already have."

"We are inviting you to participate with us in a meditative exploration designed to contribute to the evolution of consciousness," Theandos explained. "Shortly we will gather with select priests, priestesses and others from throughout the realms. The women will be in the Temple of the Divine Feminine and the men in the Temple of the Divine Masculine. Ramani and I will lead the chanting and meditation in our respective temples. You will be with each of us. Our ceremonial rituals will stimulate the merging of divine consciousness with human consciousness.

"Simply follow our guidance," Ramani advised. "Remain open to whatever is occurring, and release all attachments and expectations. Surrender to what you are experiencing. Allow the process to unfold without judging it positively or negatively. Thus we can achieve optimal results."

"Our intention is to open the portal to divine consciousness in such a compelling way, many will step through it without hesitation," Theandos clarified. "That opportunity has been available all along, but it has been hidden under layers of denial, avoidance and opposition. We want to resurrect the Divine in all."

"Since you and Luke will be stand-ins for many others, you need to be both like them and not like them," commented Ramani. "You are like them in that you are in the world working, contributing and raising a family. You are not like them in that you embody divine love so profoundly you are able to merge fully with your complement, forming a union within the highest vibrational frequency.

"Grace, your simple gown represents how you are like others, and your necklace affirms how you transcend them by fully embodying the divine feminine. Luke is equally adept at embodying the divine masculine. We ask each of you to hold both energies, the ordinary and the exalted, throughout the ceremony."

"We want to enable humankind to release hatred, fear, greed, judging, manipulation, falsehood and every other way darkness clouds insight," Theandos revealed. "We can then replace those energies with joy, peace, generosity, kindness and community."

"We are in your hands. May your intentions be made manifest in far reaching ways, during the ceremony and afterwards," Luke affirmed.

We walked with Ramani and Theandos into the foyer where others had gathered. I was aware of Luke's presence beside me. I wanted to hold his hand, or better, feel his arm around my waist. But we did not touch.

Something in me resisted the idea that we were about to be separated again. I was reliving the memory of our arrival as two, when we were taken to the same temples we were about to enter again. Not far behind lurked my unceasing fear during his imprisonment.

Instinctively Luke brushed his hand against mine to offer reassurance and comfort. With his touch I felt his love pulse through me. Raising my eyes to his I said wordlessly, "I love you, my dearest Luke." He smiled back at me.

Ramani and Theandos ascended the marble steps on one side of the foyer. A gong sounded, and silence swept across the gathering like the last rays of sunset.

"First let me express our gratitude for your willingness to gather here on such short notice," commenced Theandos. "You were asked to present yourselves at the temple with no information regarding your purpose.

"We are at a crossroads in the evolution of humankind. The forces of light and dark hang in the balance. It is our intention to participate with you in an ancient ritual that will release all limitations separating people from their divinity and replace lovelessness with its opposite.

"Some of you will be helping us generate the highest vibrational frequencies that can exist without shattering materiality. Others will receive that vibration and ground it in earthly reality. Both roles are equally critical. May we be guided by divine intention."

With that, priests and priestesses prepared to lead the men and women into their respective sacred chambers in the two temples. As I was about to leave with Ramani, Luke held me in his gaze one last time. Then we parted.

∞ ∞ ∞

Ramani and I were at the head of the procession of women, twelve dozen in all. Some were priestesses; others wore plain garments like my own. They followed us silently as we left the Temple of the Divine Masculine and entered the passageways connecting it with the Temple of the Divine Feminine. Once we were within the underground walkways, Ramani led a chant. The women responded to the ancient syllables she uttered with tonal and rhythmic perfection.

As we walked and chanted, my body began to vibrate at a high frequency. I seemed to glide across the tiled tunnel floors, having no sensation that my feet were making contact with the surface immediately below them.

"Some source of grounding you're going to be!" I thought.

"Don't worry, my dear," Ramani communicated wordlessly to me. "Your cellular structure is adjusting to enable you to hold extremely high vibrational frequencies during the forthcoming ritual. The chanting is attuning your body to the frequency of the divine feminine, strengthened by the spiritual adepts in this processional.

"When we arrive at the sacred hall where we will hold the divine rites, you will be perfectly aligned with me, the women in our group and the divine feminine herself. Thus will you be able to receive what we have to share with you and assist in bringing it into full manifestation in the consciousness of all women."

I nodded, indicating I heard and understood her.

The last passageway opened onto a verdant garden. Sunlight shocked my eyes after the relative darkness of the labyrinthine course we had followed. The procession threaded its way along the garden path, up an expanse of marble steps and into a foyer leading to a sacred chamber.

Mosaics embedded in the walls, studded with glowing quartz crystals, honored the divine feminine in each of her archetypes. Altars placed throughout the room were lit by hundreds of candles. In the front of the room was an exquisite marble platform with two ornately carved gold chairs, one for Ramani and one for me. On the floor silk cushions were arranged in three circles: amethyst purple, emerald green and ruby red.

The women divided into three groups and stood behind their cushions, their hands raised in prayer as they continued to chant. Nine priestesses waiting for our arrival split into threes to assist each group. One distributed a candle to each person, one a rose and the third was carrying a lit candle. When the roses and tapers had been handed out, three priestesses approached Ramani and me. We were given a taper, then a rose. The priestess with the lighted candle waited for the proper moment to draw near.

"May the light of the Divine shine in the spirits of everyone present here," intoned Ramani. "May it extend beyond these three circles, which include forty-eight women each, one hundred forty-four collectively, here to worship the divine feminine as she resides throughout Creation. May our love be a catalyst for the rebirth of divine light across the shared consciousness of humanity."

The third priestess approached Ramani and lit her candle, then mine. She returned to her circle and lit all forty-eight candles, while the other two priestesses with flaming candles lit those held by the women in their circles.

Ramani's chant resonated within my chest. My body filled to overflowing with light, and my heart opened like a blossom in the sun. I surrendered to the power pulsing through me. My capacity to be a vessel of divine light seemed to expand infinitely.

I became all women, all beings derived from the divine feminine, all the creative potential that existed in the world. As the chanting escalated, I integrated the divine imperative of the feminine. I asserted that all women release barriers to their sacred being and embrace their own limitless potential. I merged with feminine consciousness. Nothing was left of me as an individual woman.

Gradually the intensity of the chanting diminished, and my awareness slowly returned to my body. When I was back completely, I opened my eyes and saw what looked like three glorious jewels glistening in the room: an amethyst, an emerald and a ruby. Each circle glowed with the incandescent shades of the cushions, and the chanting women emanated a brilliant light of their own.

Ramani held up the rose and spoke with the voice of the divine feminine herself: "Divine light without divine love is incomplete. The feminine without the masculine cannot merge in perfect complementarity. Just as the feminine has the capacity to create, she cannot do so without the contribution of the masculine. The rose symbolizes the union of the two: masculine and feminine, catalyst and creative potential, male and female. May every union be one of love, unconditional, unhesitating, eternal and ultimately divine."

The fragrance of fresh roses infused the chamber. It was that of pure divine love.

Then Ramani chanted with a seductive timbre and earthly rhythms. The chamber filled with the vibration of the sensual interplay between masculine and feminine, the eternal dance toward oneness. I was sexually charged, overtaken by one long, ecstatic orgasm. At the moment of my release, my spirit left my body and flew to meet Luke.

Above us was a pyramid of light. We came together with such force all separateness was lost in our union. We became one spirit, rising beyond the apex where the vibrational frequency transcended materiality. We were swept even beyond our oneness, into all-loving divine light.

We existed beyond time. It could have been two seconds, two days or two years. Eventually we did return to our togetherness in love, then to our loving separateness, then to our physical bodies in the two temples.

Even after I returned as Grace, Luke was more fully integrated within me. A contented wholeness unavailable to me earlier existed in my heart.

Ramani chanted soothing melodies that sent me into sweet reverie. I remained in a meditative state, grateful for the opportunity just to be. By the end of it I was thoroughly revitalized and ready to take on whatever life presented to me. I was completely Grace again, with subtle whispers of Luke within. But mostly, I seemed to be a better version of myself.

Ramani arose from her chair, and I followed her lead. Our processional moved around the periphery of the chamber, honoring the feminine at each altar. Then we formed one large circle, candles aglow.

Ramani declared, "May the transformation that occurred here bring the divine feminine fully and lovingly into the lives of all women on Earth. May they carry their divinity into eternity."

Ramani led the processional in the formation of a figure eight, the symbol of infinity. Candles flickered, creating a dynamic, flowing vision of the possible: as above, so below – heaven on Earth.

After moving through eight figure eights, Ramani returned to the front of the chamber and concluded the ceremony with these words: "Beloved sisters, I am grateful to you for your abiding commitment to serve the divine feminine with all that you are. Today we strengthened the potential for perfect complementarity. May all be reborn into their divine essence. May they remember, embrace and celebrate their Source. Peace and joy to you, my dear ones."

Ramani departed majestically from the room. I followed her. I may not have been majestic, but I knew I would never be the same.

In Ramani's private quarters, I was drinking a refreshing goblet of honeyed lemon juice when I noticed something hot around my neck. Involuntarily my hand touched my necklace, which was radiating heat.

"I was wondering when you would feel the intensity of the quartz crystals glowing around your neck," Ramani said smiling. "That's a sure sign you are back. Now you can be reunited with Luke."

"Thank you for releasing me into my origins in the divine feminine. You have transformed my life, and hopefully the world. I am at your service without condition," I vowed.

"My dear, it took all of us." Ramani replied. "Even if we succeeded today, we must continue our devotions and ceremonies. Rest assured I will call on you often before my days are done. I can see us far into the future, continuing our worship of the feminine even if our temple is a grove of trees and our gowns are of the crudest homespun."

Ramani paused, contemplative, as if she were experiencing a vision of a distant place in a not so distant time. I wondered if it matched the one I had of us leaving the island just before it was destroyed.

"To the garden, dearest Grace, where once again your beloved awaits," Ramani announced. She kissed me on both cheeks and departed.

I tiptoed behind Luke sitting by a fountain and planted a kiss on the top of his head. "I never get a chance to do this," I said cheerfully, "even though you are constantly kissing me here. It is high time I dipped into my quota of top-of-the-head kisses!"

"As opposed to tip of the nose kisses, which you are very good at, by the way," Luke retorted, "or eyelid kisses, which are as soft as a butterfly's wings."

He turned around, grabbed me by the waist, lifted me up, placed me on his lap and kissed me soulfully. I wanted him urgently. Something deep within me demanded to be one with him in all ways, starting with the physical. I was considering whether a canopy of bamboo would provide shelter enough for us to make love in the garden, when a soft voice interrupted our kisses.

"We have prepared a room for you," announced a priestess. "Follow me, if you will."

I stood up, legs as shaky as a young colt's. Luke held me close. She led us down a portico lined with arches and through an ornate wooden door into a room aglow with candles and incense. A hot bath in a recessed marble tub had been prepared. Alabaster pots of essential oils and creams infused with flower essences lined one side of the tub, and drying sheets were stacked at the end. Fresh clothing was hanging on golden hooks, although I doubted we would be donning the garments anytime soon. A decanter of wine sat on a table, along with two pounded silver goblets, figs, cheese and bread.

"We should eat something," Luke said, a grin consuming his face, "so we have energy to sustain the activities I have in mind."

"Oh, really?" I challenged playfully. "A bath requires very little energy, and getting dressed afterwards can be accomplished with no effort at all."

As Luke poured the wine, he teased, "You were overly frisky in the garden, much to my mortification. A sip of wine will calm you down so you don't get too rambunctious before the night is over. I need to sleep long hours in the serenity of this peaceful place."

"And I'm going to make sure you sleep very little, if at all," I asserted, taking the goblet he offered me. "To our glorious, outrageous, marvelous, phenomenal, delicious, delirious love!"

"To my glorious, outrageous, marvelous, phenomenal, delicious, delirious Grace!" toasted Luke. We drank the wine like water after days of drought.

Luke took the goblet from my hand and set it on the table. Embracing me, he whispered, "My dear Grace, you are the only love I will ever know. If I live a hundred lifetimes, I will love only you. If we are apart for endless moments between lifetimes, I will love only you. If you are here and I am there, or if I am here and you are there, I will love only you. My love is eternal; our oneness is infinite."

We kissed, holding each other close. I leaned into him as I so loved to do, swimming in his kisses. I wanted to go slowly, to have Luke explore every mound and crevasse of my body. But I also wanted to reach the heights of ravishing ecstasy, to lose myself in oneness with him yet again.

Luke interrupted my reverie. "Shall we have that bath?"

"Only if you don't become so relaxed from a good, long soak your only desire is to take a nap," I warned with a smile.

"I have decidedly different plans," he declared, easing me into the tub.

As the water enveloped me, the fragrance of roses captured my senses. Luke rubbed rose oil into my shoulders, kneading away the tension then massaging me all over. We spent a long while in that luxurious sunken bath, coming together in languorously sensual ways. The frankincense burning in the braziers intoxicated me. I floated against Luke's body, beyond time, beyond my own mortality.

We kissed – long, slow, deep kisses that felt as if they went all the way inside. I wrapped my legs around his waist and brought him deeper into me.

"May we always find each other in this way," I said, half in prayer. "Promise me you will perpetually know me in love."

"I will find you, and when we make love I will know you are my eternal one," Luke whispered.

"Throughout lifetimes," I murmured.

"Throughout lifetimes," he vowed.

"Until we are one again," I affirmed, kissing him tenderly.

"Until we are one forever," he responded, clasping his arms around me and kissing me with devastating passion.

We slept not a wink that night, choosing instead to love each other in every conceivable way. Whatever befell us, in that lifetime or any others, our love would define our existence. And beyond incarnations, when our spirits were flying free of limitation, we would maintain our oneness indefinitely, affirming at the most fundamental yet profound level the power of love.

∞ ∞ ∞

Luke was selected to lead the institute after it was cleansed of the corrupt influences that desecrated the lives of so many. Brain implants were removed and people were brought back to relative health at the healing center I opened. Previously damaged individuals gradually recaptured their physical, psychological and spiritual wellbeing as they received numerous herbal ministrations and countless bowls of soup.

We worked together at the institute for many years, healing broken bodies and bringing lost souls back to their divinity. It was rewarding, fulfilling duty, seeing so many recover from the horrible betrayals they had endured.

As Anna and Jesse grew older, they assisted at the institute. Jesse became a compassionate counselor, Anna empowered women and girls, and Erika continued to teach. They made it possible for many to return to the outside world with strength, self-confidence and capability.

Anna and Jesse's involvement at the institute also provided an opportunity for them to explore their own relationship. They became aware of the process of splitting one spirit into two and worked with those who underwent the split as children. Along the way they helped heal the psychological wounding that resulted.

One evening when they were about sixteen years old we were discussing a particularly difficult situation they were dealing with. An adolescent boy and girl who experienced a split ten years earlier thought of themselves as brother and sister but insisted on becoming lovers. No one could convince them that was inappropriate.

Anna took the discussion further. "Jesse and I had the same thing happen to us when we were young, but we treat each other as siblings. Why can't they?"

"They love each other in another way as well," I replied. "They want to recreate oneness – who they were before the split."

"But they can't do that!" Anna insisted. "It's not right."

"Why not?" Jesse intervened. "Those who say it is wrong have no credibility with me."

Stunned, Anna shot back, "Is that what you want?"

Jesse took a deep breath and responded from the heart. "Yes, but I know it's not possible. I love you more than I can ever love another, and I am also aware I would lose you if I treated you as anyone other than my sister. I am at peace with that."

We waited for Anna to respond, but she was uncharacteristically speechless.

Luke filled the void. "You just described the most unfortunate and painful consequence of your split as children. When we brought you into our family, we anticipated that some day you might feel as Jesse does. But you were so young, the only alternative was to raise you as brother and sister.

"Grace and I were adults when the split occurred. We had the freedom and maturity to become lovers. You two did not, which is beyond unfortunate. Jesse, you have struggled with conflicting feelings and chosen to love and respect Anna as your sister. Bless you for that. Grace and I apologize to you both for any difficulty or confusion we might have caused."

"No apologies are needed," Anna declared. "You loved us from the moment we met and saved us from a terrible fate. You are our parents and we are family. That is my truth.

"Jesse, I love you more than anyone in the world, and I can't imagine life without you. But you are my brother. Nothing more. I hope you understand."

"I do," Jesse affirmed. "Which is why I am grateful to have you as my sister."

"I knew you two were remarkable," I commented. "But this conversation helped me recognize how deeply aware you have become. I love and respect you all the more."

"A prouder father doesn't exist," Luke beamed. "Come here!" We gathered in a group hug, united by our love and the unique circumstances that brought us together.

After that Anna and Jesse were more open and generous with each other. They had a shared understanding based on what they each held in their heart. The topic never arose again.

Luke and I continued to collaborate with Ramani and Theandos. *Collaborate* is an audacious word for me to use, but that's how it felt to me. The four of us were pursuing a mission together, to continue thwarting power abuse while we healed those who suffered great travesties at its hand. We did so with our capacity to resonate at the highest frequencies of divine love. Theandos and Ramani energized our efforts from the temples, and Luke and I applied them to worldly reality.

They visited us often in our home, reminiscing about the joy they had known there and experiencing more of it by becoming part of our extended family.

The children grew to adulthood in what seemed more like two years than twenty. Tomas remained his solid, steady self throughout it all, keeping the details of our lives in order without once drawing attention to himself. We were blessed, this family that now included eight of us. I couldn't imagine a more meaningful or loving life.

But all was not well among the far reaches of humanity. Dark forces retained a foothold despite concerted efforts to neutralize their influence and impact. After being nearly conquered by those who serve the light, corruption reappeared with a vengeance. We were doing good work, as were many others, but it was not enough to stop the inexorable advances of the fallen.

The mystics within the temples saw this unfolding. We were asked to heal as many people as we could and, in the meantime, prepare for possible leave-taking.

One evening as we were listening to Anna and Jesse recount what happened at the institute that day, a messenger arrived.

"You are to meet Theandos and Ramani at the dock just east of the city before dawn," he announced. "A boat will be waiting with a Merkabah painted in red on a white sail. Bring only your most essential belongings and whatever you need to start a new life elsewhere. The vessel will leave at dawn. Don't be late."

Luke stood up to address the messenger directly. "Report that we'll be there, and please express our gratitude for having received this warning and invitation. Now we must prepare to leave."

We spent a few moments after the messenger departed answering questions and calming concerns. Luke explained to Anna, Jesse, Erika and Tomas that the influence of corruption had been steadily expanding. The seers in the temples must have warned that a perilous fall from grace was imminent.

We were being given an opportunity to depart before that occurred, not because we were special or privileged, but because we had the knowledge, capability and commitment to begin anew. We would take Ramani and Theandos to safety in order to preserve the wisdom and mysticism they embodied. Through them the light of the Divine would live on. Our responsibility was to help establish a life with them in a different location.

We discussed what each person should pack for the journey, urging Anna and Jesse to release their many treasures. "Pick just a few of your most precious objects," I suggested, "and say goodbye to the rest." When I heard those words, I committed to following my own advice.

I knelt in front of the altar in our sitting room. "Please guide me to see what I should take with me," I prayed. I was shown a small bag containing only a few items: my necklace, the box and ribbons from Luke, my journals, the dried rose from Tomas, the crystal pyramid in the apex above our bed, and my gossamer silk gown and tunic. I was wearing the ring from Luke.

I asked Tomas to gather seeds and cuttings from our garden so we could create it again wherever we landed. Erica was selecting important records of our civilization to serve as a small archive. Anna and Jesse were surprising themselves with their choices of what to bring, items with sweet memories more than anything particularly valuable.

Luke was making sure we all had enough basics to get us through any eventuality: essential clothing, extra layers for warmth, tools and implements for various purposes, and, bless him, some of the smaller, more exquisite examples of artistry and craftsmanship in the house.

We began loading a cart with supplies and baggage. Luke monitored what we each brought, to assure nothing was included that didn't absolutely warrant it. Everyone remained so calm it was almost as if we were packing for a cruise instead of an escape.

The seriousness of our task was lost on no one. But rather than being in a panic, we remained focused and methodical. Nonetheless, we had spent two decades in this extraordinary home, and now we were about to leave it forever. It was heartbreaking.

When everything was packed and we were ready to depart, Luke brought us together, holding hands in a semi-circle facing the house. "I invite each of you to say goodbye to our home, however you choose, silently or aloud," he said quietly.

We blessed the house with prayers from within. A deep sadness burst forth from me in a torrent of tears. I grieved the loss of our home and our lives as we had known them. Even more profoundly, I mourned the victory of fallen consciousness over enlightenment. Despite our efforts, we failed to right the wrongs perpetrated by the few against the many.

Everyone experienced their own private sorrow as we turned our backs on our home and headed to the dock.

∞　∞　∞

We arrived with ample time to load what we brought and settle into our quarters on the sailing ship. It was larger than I anticipated, and I wondered if we had been too conservative in our choices of what to pack.

When carts from the temples appeared full of provisions – barrels of fresh water, food and supplies – I saw the wisdom in using the ship's capacity to store what we would need to survive the voyage. No one knew where we would land or how long it would take to get there. We needed all the essentials the ship could hold.

Just before dawn Theandos and Ramani arrived along with a small entourage from the temples, five couples in all.

Ramani smiled broadly when she saw us ready to welcome them. Once the final container of goods was loaded and secured, we set sail.

Theandos introduced us to those on board. The ship's crew consisted of priests specially trained to sail the vessel and carry us to safety. Preparations for our departure had been occurring for quite a while.

Everyone else on the island was being left behind, perhaps to be annihilated before the next dawn. A dense heaviness came over me as I recalled the priestesses who participated in temple rituals and may soon be swept away. I remembered people at the institute and in my healing centers and soup shops. The enormity of what was about to happen came crashing down upon me, and I wept anew.

Hatred, violence and power abuse were so deeply embedded in society, it was no longer possible to counteract their influence or slow their progression. Conflicting forces consistently thwarted the emanations of love. Light and dark were perpetually in opposition, and the latter was winning.

Beings from the many universes stepped aside, having agreed that nothing more could be done. They were prohibited from interfering to stop the influence and actions of the fallen. A civilization corrupted to the core, beyond redemption, could not continue. It was time to allow Mother Nature to have the final say.

The island was almost out of sight when a flash of light erupted from a volcano. The explosion was so immense, I feared sparks would reach our ship and catch the sails on fire. Then an ominous rumbling arose from deep within the ocean. We went below deck and strapped ourselves securely to the hold. Massive waves crested under the ship, stalwart amidst the chaos. The island didn't survive the ocean's onslaught. An entire civilization disappeared forever.

We remained silent for a long while afterward, praying for the release of all spirits into the embrace of the Divine and forgiving those who precipitated this violent and cataclysmic fall.

When our ship entered the open ocean we came together as an extended family, a tight-knit group with a clear purpose if not absolute certainty about where it would unfold. After six weeks we saw land in sight. We had envisioned the geography of our new homeland, and we affirmed confidently this was indeed the place.

We made our home in a strange land, befriending those who had lived there for generations before us and nurturing a peaceful community with them. They helped us build a pyramid of sorts, a huge mound of dirt consecrated through the course of many rituals conducted on and within it. Families from all over came to witness the ceremonies at our makeshift temple, astounded by what they labeled the "magic" that occurred, which was simply the manifestation of divine light and love.

This was later known as the Tor in Glastonbury, but to us it was our temple.

The divine wisdom the priests and priestesses carried to this new homeland created a strong vortex of positive intention. Everyone and everything thrived.

Tomas' plants grew as never before, the seeds taking root in the rich black soil and the seedlings finding the temperate climate conducive to their propagation. People came from far and wide to trade for his cuttings and learn his growing techniques. I taught the women how to listen to the plants, and they introduced me to their own healing remedies.

Luke and I helped build a communal farm. We learned the language of the tribes that populated the island and shared the bounty from our gardens and orchards.

Anna married a local chieftain and with their love assured peace throughout the land. Jesse became a priest, preferring not to marry. He couldn't bring himself to love anyone other than Anna.

Erika, ever the scholar, became an early anthropologist who studied local customs. Along the way she spread her teachings and was instrumental in defusing tribal conflict.

Although we worked hard, we lived in a constant state of gratitude and bliss.

My dearly beloved Luke was ever the patriarch, emissary and benevolent leader. He also remained my ardent lover. Even as we grew older, we shared precious nights of intimacy that brought us together in blessed oneness. My love for him became so woven into my being it was impossible to imagine life without him.

But the day did come when he left the Earth plane, as I knew he would. We had agreed I would follow soon thereafter, for I have no will to live without him.

And now as I prepare to lie down in our bed for the last time, alone, I must reveal important secrets to you, starting with the least significant.

First, I leave my necklace, that it may continue to emanate divine light throughout the ages.

Second, I leave the box and ribbons, with the ring inside. I do so that I might find them again, should that be appropriate.

Third, I leave my journals. Reading the entries on the ship as we made our journey, I was struck by the extent to which they portended with precision and insight everything that would happen in my life. I vow to continue writing throughout lifetimes and make my stories available to others, filling their hearts with love.

Finally, the most precious legacy of all is my conviction that there exists nothing but love. Recognize it in the faces of those around you. See it in the gifts from Nature that constantly grace your lives. Feel it in your heart when you are filled with contrary emotions, perhaps most especially then.

Commit to being love in every way you can. Choose love over all other alternatives. Know you begin in love and end in love. And when you lie down to take your last breath, you will do so in peace.

GRACE'S HEALING SOUP

To nurture, love and live in greater harmony

Ingredients
1 tbsp. butter
1 quart vegetable broth
1 chopped onion
1 pound of potatoes, cut into pieces
1 pound of Brussels sprouts, halved
½ pound shiitake mushrooms. sliced
1 minced garlic clove
1 inch minced fresh ginger
1 tsp. turmeric
1 tsp. fennel
1 tsp. Himalayan salt
Anything else that strikes your fancy

Directions
Use the freshest locally sourced organic produce if it is available
Prepare the ingredients with love in your heart, thanking each one for its precious contribution
In a heavy pot sauté chopped onion in butter until translucent and golden
Add broth, vegetables and spices
Simmer over a low flame for one hour with your favorite music playing
Taste the soup and add whatever will make it over-the-top delicious
Simmer for another half hour while you set the table as you sing
Serve with joy and gratitude

ACKNOWLEDGEMENTS

For the past half century I have been blessed to be part of a constantly emerging, joyfully celebratory sisterhood. Each of these dear friends exhibits the divine feminine in all of her unhesitating acceptance, generous support and unconditional love. They are, in alphabetical order:

Susan Blake

Delinda Chapman

Linda Davidson

Choong Gaian

Davida Hartman

Sally Hudson

Trudie London

Sharon Mehdi

Regina Meredith

Pix Morgan

Sandra Tripp

Justine Turner

Wendy Weir

Explore additional books by Gates McKibbin at
www.lovehopegive.com

Epic Steps: *Rekindling Democracy, Unity and Peace*

One, Beyond Time
Love, 24 AD
Hope, 120 AD
Give, 1671 AD

The Light in the Living Room: *Dad's Messages from the Other Side*

Lovelines: *Notes from Spirit on Loving and Being Loved*

A Course in Courage: *Disarming the Darkness with Strength of Heart*

A Handbook on Hope: *Fusing Optimism and Action*

The Life of the Soul: *The Path of Spirit in Your Lifetimes*

Available Wisdom: *Insights from Beyond the Third Dimension*

Forging Faith: *Direct Experience of the Divine*

Made in United States
North Haven, CT
14 August 2022